THE SAINT AND THE PEOPLE IMPORTERS

LESLIE CHARTERIS

SERIES EDITOR: IAN DICKERSON

THOMAS & MERCER

Published by Thomas & Mercer, Seattle

www.apub.com

ISBN-13: 9781477843024
ISBN-10: 1477843027

Cover design by David Drummond, www.salamanderhill.com

Printed in the United States of America.

PUBLISHER'S NOTE

The text of this book has been preserved from the original edition and includes vocabulary, grammar, style, and punctuation that might differ from modern publishing practices. Every care has been taken to preserve the author's tone and meaning, allowing only minimal changes to punctuation and wording to ensure a fluent experience for modern readers.

FOREWORD TO THE NEW EDITION

It's funny the things you remember from your childhood. I was a kid when I first read this book and four things about it have remained with me: the title itself has a heck of an impact. Whereas other Saint adventures of the time had the more pedestrian moniker of *Catch the Saint* or *Send for the Saint*, importing people seemed like a desperately heinous crime, particularly to young me in the 1970s. It still seems the same to a somewhat older me in the twenty-first century but of course now, sadly, it's become a lot more common place.

And then there was the opening—Simon Templar going for a curry (and no, that's not a spoiler!). I'm not entirely sure why this remains with me. Sure, it jars somewhat with the Saint's previously documented more refined tastes, but Charteris loved a good curry, so there's no reason to think the Saint wouldn't.

Then there are the characters. Charteris always sprinkled his books with a wonderful collection of characters for the Saint to interact with, whether it be Sheriff Haskins from *The Saint in Miami*, or the likes of Inspector Fernack, Chief Inspector Teal, and Hoppy Uniatz from far too many Saint books to list here. He always had fun with his characters and the same stands true for this novel, with Kalki, Short Wave, and even Fowler adding to the army of Saintly foes.

But what I first think of when I recall this book is a newspaper headline featured within it. Don't worry, I won't quote it, for it would be giving away some of the plot (although previous editions featured it as part of the back cover blurb). But there's a little section early on in the story which I read and reread as a kid, and it made me appreciate the value of each and every word that I read and write.

It's funny the impact a book can have.

Anyway, get ready, for I think Simon Templar is about to go for a curry . . .

—Ian Dickerson

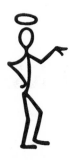

THE SAINT AND THE PEOPLE IMPORTERS

PREFACE

This is another of those joint efforts which I initiated with *The Saint on TV*, and which were accepted well enough to be followed by three other titles of similarly mixed parentage.

In this case, however, there are a few small differences. I first suggested the basic theme to Fleming Lee, who wanted to try his hand at a TV script. He worked out a synopsis, in which I made some suggestions, and which I passed on to the TV producers with my approval. Typically, this was not good enough for them: they bought his synopsis, but would not let him work on the script, and turned it over to another writer, eventually ending up with a script in which our original elements were barely recognisable.

Later, I suggested to Fleming that he should draft this book version, but revert to our original outline, ignoring the television "improvements." Which he did, at the same time incorporating some slight changes of my own. Finally, as with all the preceding experiments of this kind, I personally revised the whole manuscript, doing my best to see that the style conformed as closely as possible to my own.

Once again, then, this should not be classed as a "ghosted" job, since I give full credit to my assistant. But since I have also had my own hand in it from start to finish, I don't think it is being offered to Saint fans under false pretences.

—Leslie Charteris (1971)

CHAPTER ONE:

HOW SIMON TEMPLAR READ ABOUT ALI, AND HIS CURRY WAS DELAYED

1

The identity of the passenger who left his evening paper behind in a certain London taxi one dull September afternoon will probably never be discovered: he passed through this world but once, and may have nothing else in the course of his transit that will ever concern posterity. But the newspaper was still lying there on the seat when Simon Templar hailed the cab on Jermyn Street behind Fortnum & Mason's, within which epicurean supermarket he had just concluded a transaction involving several thousand sturgeon eggs, and thus has a fair claim to have been the starting point of this adventure.

Simon Templar had long ago given up trying to predict where Adventure would come from: his only certainty was that he could never escape it. He would stumble upon it, or it would trip over him, but one way or another they were fated to come together, by the same kind of destiny that had ordained perhaps as a symbol for that afternoon, that Mr Fortnum should be forever linked with Mr Mason.

There had been an era long ago, admittedly, when Simon Templar had gone more than halfway to meet this agreeable doom. With an imagination as unlimited as possibility itself he had set out on his hunt;

his territory was the world and his prey the two-legged predators who fattened on other men's toil and hopes and sufferings: extortioners, swindlers, racketeers—every manner of human parasite that crept on the scalp of the earth, and especially those who had burdened themselves with a weighty enough load of ill-gotten gold to warrant the attention of a man of Simon's expensive tastes.

But while a fair share of the wealth he rescued from the coffers of the Ungodly found its way into his own bank accounts, a large proportion of it ended up back in the hands of its original rightful owners. This fact, combined with Simon's penchant for extralegal action and his contempt for the creaky wheels of due process, had caused some historically attuned pen-pusher to dub him the Robin Hood of Modern Crime. The comparison was apt, but another shorter and more mysteriously ambivalent sobriquet had attached itself to him very early in his career and had soon all but replaced his real name in the public mind.

It was a *nom de guerre* heard by detective officers and bandit chieftains with equal unease: The Saint.

More recently, he claimed that he positively leaned sideways in a noble effort to avoid trouble, but with no more success than an unskilful matador attempting to evade an educated bull. Their mutual karma was bigger than both of them. And that afternoon where we came in was a fair sample of its working.

Having directed the driver to take him to the Hilton Hotel, where he had no more nefarious objective in mind than the inhibition of a cool quenching rum punch in Trader Vic's air-conditioned basement, the Saint pushed the abandoned newspaper out of his way, and settled back to relax while he was ferried through dense shoals of rush-hour traffic. The newspaper lay ignored beside him as he crossed his legs, folded his arms, and watched the crowds rushing along the sidewalks in a last-minute push to spend as much of their money as possible before the last shops closed, or to catch a homeward bus or train before everyone else with the same idea got ahead of them.

Even among those elegantly draped though unseemly hurrying West End throngs, Simon Templar had stood out as an extraordinarily well-tailored, handsome, and striking man. His six feet two inches, honed to balanced perfection through hard and steady use, set him above most of his fellow-creatures in stature as well as in fitness, and his blue eyes blazed in his tanned face with a magically startling translucency. Even the way he carried himself was unusual, somehow combining the urbane poise of an idle aristocrat with the quiet watchful readiness of a jungle-fighter.

Nature's lavish kindness to the Saint, included the visual acuity of a jet pilot, and also burdened him with a ceaseless curiosity about everything that it took in. Long before his taxi turned from Piccadilly into Clarges Street, his eye had been caught during the cab's frequent pauses in the inevitable jams by those hand-lettered, forcefully worded broadsheets which London's newspaper vendors hang on their small red or yellow stands. There was such a journalistic entrepreneur on almost every corner—an invariably afflicted-looking man in stained cap and shapeless shoes—and ordinarily the Saint would not have found his imagination stirred by even their most lurid promises.

He could pass by "Cigarette Tax Shock" without a glance. "Dock Strike Chaos" was such a commonplace that it would have blended indiscernibly with the pavement and the shop fronts. Even "Au Pair Girl Murder! Pictures!," which could be counted on to galvanise weary commuters into a veritable stampede towards the news-hawkers with coins thrust forward in impatient hands, and to hold them spellbound on an underground ride from Piccadilly Circus to Maida Vale, would not have produced even a responsive tremor in the Saint's vital organs.

But "Pakistani Crucified In Soho" rang with such a brazen barbaric resonance that even the Saint's well-tempered nervous system could not entirely resist its call.

"Pakistani Crucified In Soho!"

The message was echoed and repeated as Simon's taxi made its way in halts and spurts of sudden speed towards the hazy green of Hyde Park and the sunset-reddened glassy tower of the Hilton Hotel. In his imagination he saw the Pakistani's exotic fate proclaimed before the department stores of Oxford Street, made loudly known along the Strand, and writ large on every corner of Trafalgar Square. The whole of the West End was aquiver with the ghastly tidings, and vast ant-streams of rail-borne commuters were even now pouring out into the countryside to spread the word to Croydon, Tunbridge Wells, and Beaconsfield.

The Saint's immunity was not total. While he was not curious enough to have stopped his driver so that he could buy a newspaper, he was too intrigued to resist the impulse to pick up the secondhand tabloid that happened to be lying beside him. But before unfurling it he paused to wonder cynically if he might after all be cheated. Perhaps the editor of this particular journal had suffered a lapse in his sense of values or a misjudgment of public taste and had left the unfortunate Pakistani out of his columns altogether, assuming that the devaluation of some Latin American currency or the murder of a refugee by Russian border guards were matters more worthy of public knowledge?

Simon unfolded the discarded paper and was not disappointed. The Pakistani's lot was emblazoned across the top of the front page in a barrage of letters two inches high. Below, in small but still bold type, were details calculated to funnel the reader's eye down into the morass of finer print that made up the body of the sheet: "*Waiter in Soho restaurant nailed to garage wall . . . dead when discovered this morning . . . believed to be victim of immigrant smuggling gang . . .*"

Simon's eye scanned the column from "*Grim sight greeted bobbies*" through "*Shopkeeper heard groans*" to "*Did he threaten to talk?*"

The unpleasant details of the Pakistani's demise and the subsequent discovery of his spread-eagled body in a temporarily vacant garage held less interest for the Saint than another fact which made him stop and look again when he was about two thirds of the way down the page:

> *"The murdered man was a waiter at the Golden Crescent Restaurant in Soho, where his Pakistani colleagues claimed to know little about him or his origins."*

Simon lowered his foundling journal and leaned forward. The narrow centre panel in the glass partition that separated driver from passenger was already partially lowered. The Saint spoke through the opening.

"I don't think I'll stop at the Hilton after all," he said. "I've developed a sudden craving for curry. Do you think we can get to the Golden Crescent Restaurant before midnight even in this traffic? It's on Newlin Street, near Leicester Square."

The driver was a small ageing ugly man with a pocked nose and a surprisingly cheerful disposition.

"We can try," he said over his shoulder. "If you're in a hurry, there's a hundred other curry houses, and with all respect I don't see how anybody can tell 'em apart unless it's by the different kinds of indigestion you pick up from the . . ."

Simon was spared any more of his chauffeur's culinary comments when the current log-jam of cars broke into motion again.

"I think I'll make it the Golden Crescent just the same," he said. "I've been there before. *De gustibus,* et cetera . . ."

"Righto," the driver answered tolerantly. "Leicester Square it is."

"And no hurry," said the Saint.

"Don't worry."

The driver shifted very audibly into second gear. Simon let himself be jolted back into his seat again and got on with his study of the evening's news. The front page treatment of the Pakistani's death was more visceral than analytical, but at the bottom of the column, in bold print, was a promising announcement:

> *EXCLUSIVE! HOW ILLEGAL IMMIGRANTS FALL PREY TO EXTORTION GANG. THE INSIDE STORY, BY TAM ROWAN. SEE PAGE 3.*

The Saint saw page three. His driver, in the meantime, was beginning a series of torturous manoeuvres through clogged streets that would eventually enable him to get to Simon's new destination. The tide of the evening rush was in full flood now. Pedestrians pressed toe to heel on the sidewalks, and the earth trembled to the surge of trains through the subterranean labyrinths.

It was understandable, Simon thought, that men of the Asian lands who wanted to avail themselves in person of Britain's advantages ran into British objections and were forced to take unofficial routes into the country, thereby putting themselves in the category of "illegal immigrants." It would seem to anybody observing mid-London late on a weekday afternoon that the island of which it was the capital not only had no room for new inhabitants, but in fact was about to founder under the weight of the ones who were already there.

Simon shut his eyes and ears to the throngs outside his taxi and concentrated on Tam Rowan's exclusive inside story, which got off the mark with a verbal ring: *"I was threatened with death for writing this article."*

Mr Rowan, it seemed, had taken a professional interest in illegal immigration for some time past, and now had finally managed to introduce his proboscis into circles so touchy about their privacy that they had anonymously offered to detach not only his inquisitive sniffer but also his whole head if he did not lay off immediately.

Rowan revealed these facts in dramatic, rather breathless terms not wholly unflattering to himself, and then got down to a disappointingly vague account of what he had found out in the course of his snooping. The Saint's impression was that Tam Rowan was not quite as heroically indifferent to the well-being of his highly active nose as he made himself out to be, and that he knew a lot more than he was willing to spill in *The Evening Record*. Much of what he said was common knowledge: large numbers of people, especially from Pakistan and India, wanted to come to Britain. Britain, for obvious reasons, could not accommodate and offer jobs to any but a small proportion of those non-Britons who wanted to immigrate. The British government had been forced to restrict the human influx by means of annual quota systems, and to further refine the screening process by giving priority to new arrivals who practised some profession or had some skill that would make them an asset instead of an unemployable liability to the society they wanted to enter. A Pakistani doctor could get in with no trouble. A Pakistani labourer or clerk, to whom the wages of a London Transport ticket collector would have seemed comparable to the wealth of Midas, had almost no chance at all of entering.

It was those with no special qualifications for entry, and who were refused the vital employment permit, who sometimes decided to have a try at getting in anyway. Transportation, by plane to France or Benelux and thence by boat to a deserted stretch of English coast, was the usual method. Fraudulent documents of every necessary kind could be obtained in advance for stunning prices, and once ashore the smuggled man could lose himself so completely that the government authorities admitted that they had almost no chance of locating such an offender after he was inside the country's borders.

The illegal immigrant, however, did not feel as secure as the government's pessimistic attitude might seem to have warranted. And that was the crux of the racket the Saint was reading about. A gang of blackmailers was raking in a rich profit from fearful, uninformed, often ignorant Pakistanis and Indians who had sneaked into the country and were vulnerable to threats of exposure. Among the blackmailers were some of the Asians' own countrymen—and to increase the unsavoury irony, the extortion syndicate got rich both coming and going, since they ran a two-sided business and many of the people they blackmailed were men they had helped slip into England in the first place, thus ingeniously providing themselves with a prelocated flock of sheep for shearing.

Simon did not at all admire illegal immigration nor the people who indulged in it, but he admired blackmailers even less. He was not a sentimental man, and he could appreciate an audacious bit of thievery with the taste of a connoisseur. He could enjoy the pricking of the pompous rich—though it was the pompous part and not the rich part that he disliked—and he could relish a duel between equals. But blackmail, by its very nature, had always struck him as especially rotten, and a blackmailer who sucked the blood of poor and defenceless people seemed to him to exist on a level approximately equivalent to the underside of a cockroach.

Simon folded the newspaper and tucked it into the pocket of his raincoat with the pleasant feeling of being no longer at loose ends but instead of having set a clear course in a promising direction. His driver was not so fortunate. In trying to take a shortcut through Soho he finally got himself bogged down near Wardour Street off Brewer Street. Here, in a notorious backwater bottleneck behind the theatre and restaurant district, the traffic jam seemed to be nearing the oft-predicted urban millennium when the only solution will be to cover the whole mess with concrete and start all over again on top of it.

"I'll walk from here," Simon said through the opening in the glass partition.

He got out and paid the driver.

"There's plenty of curry restaurants around here," the cabman said. "Must be at least one in every block."

"I think I'll go to the Golden Crescent anyway," Simon told him. "They may all use the same brand of chutney, but where I'm going there's something special about the atmosphere."

2

To the uninitiated foreigner, London is Big Ben, double-decker buses, dazzling uniforms, and Buckingham Palace. The contrivers of English tourist brochures tend to give the central section of the city called Soho the same treatment that a respectable family gives to a fallen female relative: they get a kick out of knowing about her but they don't go out of their way to advertise her existence very exuberantly to outsiders. Appropriately heralded by the statue of Eros in the middle of Piccadilly Circus on its southwest corner, Soho is a roughly rectangular area of about ninety acres bounded on the north by Oxford Street and on the east by Charing Cross Road, but its distinction is much more a matter of atmosphere than of physical boundaries.

Soho is, in the most far-reaching sense of the word, an entertainment district. It contains Carnaby Street, the birthplace of a contemporary form of sartorial extravagance, which for some tastes would be entertainment enough, but that is only one facet of its resources. Along its many-angled, space-starved streets and alleys the stalwart sensation-seeker can visit a pub, a penny arcade, a bookmaker's shop, or a strip-tease show. He can buy a red hot magazine or a blue hot reel of movie film. He can eat at an Indian, Chinese, French, German, Italian, Balkan, American, Jewish, or even an English restaurant. He can get himself an expensive companion in an expensive bar, or a cheap dancing partner, or a souvenir lump on the back of his skull if he should be foolhardy enough to follow the wrong helpful little chap into the wrong obscure doorway.

Soho, regarded (for literary effect) as a painted woman, is considerably cleaner, better dressed, and brighter than what might loosely be called her counterparts in other great cities. When the Saint got out of his taxi he was standing in front of a pub as staid and wholesome as any in Oxford or Windsor. Many of the passers-by would have looked at home on the most pristine boulevard in Belgravia.

But Soho, being the sort of place it is, attracts in large numbers that curious variety of human being who combines an enterprising spirit with inordinate laziness and a total lack of moral-principle. If prevented by circumstances from becoming a politician or a fiction-writer, such an individual will tend to gravitate to the kind of sub-surface sources of income with which Soho abounds. The Saint saw a female of the species almost as soon as he left the kerb and set off down a short, constricted side street. She was fat and young and had curly black hair, and she was sitting in a ground floor window of a building across the road. When she saw Simon her expression of disconsolate boredom did not change, but remarkably like a clockwork toy she raised one plumpish hand and mechanically beckoned to him three times with a pudgy forefinger.

The Saint cheerfully tipped an imaginary hat and strode on. Turning into the next, more populous street, he ran a gauntlet of second rate strip-show establishments whose wares were vividly publicised by a fusillade of glossy photographs on either side of their doors—photographs whose charming bare subjects had no connection whatever with the dancing girls presumably on non-stop view inside. He edged around a ragged stoop-shouldered vendor of hot chestnuts, passed a hamburger house, a magazine shop, and an Italian delicatessen, and turned down to Shaftesbury Avenue, which was roaring with traffic and jammed with sightseers. He had to wait at a corner until he could get across the avenue to its southern side. The glow of the setting sun stained the façades of all the buildings a livid red. The day had seemed perfectly clear, but now that the sun had sunk below the roof-tops an autumn haze was filtering and deepening the tone of the light. As Simon continued on towards the Golden Crescent, he almost suddenly became aware of a wintry chill in the air, as if the sinking of the sun had revealed an underlying coldness that had been there all the time.

Or was the chill inside him—an omen of events that every deliberate step was bringing nearer?

He was approaching the Indian restaurant from its rear, and he could smell the exotic pungency of its kitchen exhaust while he was still yards away. The restaurant was on a corner, and behind it and its neighbouring shops ran a narrow alley serving their back doors. Simon would not have paid any particular attention to a medium-sized van which had backed into the alley if he had not happened to notice the two men who apparently were in charge of it. Their appearance was so startling that he paused and glanced at the side-panels of the blue van expecting to see the advertisement for a circus.

Instead he saw the words: "Supreme Imports Ltd., Purveyors of Finest Indian Foodstuffs."

All in a matter of seconds, he was able to take another look at the men who had attracted his attention as they lifted a crate and cartons from inside the van and carried them into the back door of the Golden Crescent. Both of them wore dirty blue workmen's clothes, but that was where any resemblance ended.

By far the more striking of the two was a giant Indian or Pakistani, at least six and a half feet tall, with muscles and girth to match his amazing stature. The huge dome of his skull was bald, like a great gleaming egg resting in the bristling black nest of muttonchop whiskers and jutting moustaches which smothered the lower regions of his head. The bridge of his nose receded abnormally as it approached his massive brow, and his little oily eyes gave the impression of having rolled down close together in the depression like a pair of black ball-bearings.

The small cramped jet eyes fastened on Simon's face for an instant and then flicked away to concentrate on the business of moving the wooden crate into the restaurant's storeroom.

The other member of the blue-clad team was a European, and in no way as remarkable as his mate. It was just that his unusual smallness—jockey-like, the Saint thought—was so emphasised by the monstrous Indian's Brobdingnagian bulk that he looked like a pigmy in comparison. He was not only rather short, but also thin, with an anxious death's-head face surmounted by a closely cut crop of coarse hair that stood rigidly up on end. He blinked rapidly as he worked, and did not notice Simon as the Saint went on past the entrance of the alley.

The Saint had no reason to think any more—for the time being—about the two oddly assorted purveyors of finest Indian foodstuffs. He was much more interested in knowing what the owner and staff of the Golden Crescent could tell him about their compatriots' problems—if not their own—of involvement with extortioners of the kind whose bloody deed had just made the headlines.

Simon knew the Golden Crescent through half a dozen visits he had made during the past year. The only thing which differentiated it from scores of other Indian restaurants in London (distinction between Indian and Pakistani cuisine being virtually nonexistent in the British public mind) was the intensely calorific excellence of its curried lamb and the benevolent hospitality of its proprietor, Abdul Haroon. There were more lavish, and possibly better, Indian restaurants, but there was none with a more sociable and talkative owner—and talkativeness was a quality for which the Saint felt a keen desire on this particular evening.

He rounded the corner and approached the restaurant's modest front entrance, an ordinary glass door flanked on either side by plate-glass windows, each bearing in appropriately gilt lettering the words "Golden Crescent Restaurant." Above the door, so that it could be seen by prospective customers approaching from east or west, hung another gilded announcement of the restaurant's identity. It seemed unlikely that even the most unobservant pedestrian could feel any doubt that he was, indeed, at the portals of the Golden Crescent, but in case there should be any last-minute doubts among the exceptionally dull-witted the fact was confirmed once more by neat gold lettering on the glass of the entrance door itself.

Mr Abdul Haroon was loquacious even in his advertising.

Before going inside, the Saint glanced through one of the windows, over a row of sickly ferns which had somehow survived the sunless and spice-laden atmosphere of the interior. It was barely six o'clock, and he was glad to see that he would be the first customer to arrive that evening.

He opened the door and stepped in. There was no entrance alcove, and he was immediately in the midst of white-covered tables packed as close together as sheep in an overcrowded fold. Along the walls were red-yellowish lamps and hand-painted murals of imaginative Eastern landscapes in which all the trees were palms and all the buildings were variations on the Taj Mahal. To the right in the rear was a small but well-stocked bar. A passageway led past the bar to the kitchen and cloakrooms.

The first thing the Saint's senses registered as he entered was the wonderful smell of the place, dominated at the moment by cloves and saffron. The second fact that struck him was that there was not a single waiter in sight.

He tried to close the air-cushioned door as noisily as possible behind him, and picked out a table where he would be able to sit with his back to the wall and see the entrance, the bar, and the passage that gave access to the back rooms. Before he could take a seat a waiter, already known to him from previous visits as Mahmud, came rushing out around the bar from the inner sanctuary, jerking the hem of his white jacket into place over his baggy Eastern trousers.

"I am so sorry, sir!" he was exclaiming. "We have just opened our door this minute."

"Not to worry," Simon said. "I'd like this table, if it's not reserved."

"Mr Templar!" the waiter said with sudden recognition.

He hurried to help Simon slip off his raincoat. "So long since you were here and no one to greet you!"

Mahmud, a Pakistani like Abdul Haroon, as his Moslem name indicated, was of moderate height, light-skinned, black-haired, and quick. He was in his early twenties and despite a professionally subservient manner gave the impression that he was destined for higher things than dishing up rice and poppadums, and knew it.

"You have a good memory," said the Saint. "It's been some time since I was here—and it was usually Ali who waited on me."

The Golden Crescent employed only three waiters and the evening paper had not made it clear which of them had been murdered. If it had been the one called Ali, a middle-aged quiet man, Mahmud gave no indication of it.

"It helps to cultivate the memory in my profession," he said with smiling complacency.

He had pulled the table away from the wall so that Simon could sit down on the banquette. Now he pushed the table back and flicked an imaginary crumb off the clean white cloth. Like most tablecloths at restaurants of the Golden Crescent's class, this one had a small but very neatly mended torn spot. It amused Simon to see the little white scar as soon as he looked to confirm his guess that it would be there—almost as much as it amused him that waiter Mahmud insisted on being completely unaware that one of his colleagues was even at this moment making grisly news posters all over London.

"Thank you," Simon said coolly. "Would you please hand me that paper from the pocket of my coat before you hang it up?"

"Of course, sir."

As the Saint took the paper he unfolded it on the table in front of him. Mahmud studiously avoided noticing the headline, but Simon refused to let him escape. When the waiter came back from hanging up the coat the Saint tapped the fat black letters.

"With your memory," he said, "you can't have forgotten Ali."

Mahmud stiffened into a rigidly formal posture.

"No, sir."

"It was the Ali who worked here then?"

"Yes, sir. Would you like a drink, sir?"

Mahmud staunchly met the Saint's eyes through an invisible barrier as thick as the armour plating of a battleship.

"I'll have a Peter Dawson with ice."

"Yes, sir," said Mahmud. "With plain water?"

The Saint nodded and smiled.

"You do have a very fine memory," he said pleasantly. "I hope as the evening goes on you'll find that it covers things other than customers' names and drinking habits."

Mahmud's face was still expressionless but he permitted his dark eyes to glance again at the newspaper.

"You are interested in this matter?"

"Yes," Simon said.

"For reasons of your own profession?"

For an instant Mahmud did not sound like a waiter.

"Possibly," said the Saint.

"Thank you, sir," Mahmud replied, sounding like a waiter again. "I will get your drink and the menu."

3

Simon realised as Mahmud walked quickly away that the waiter's sudden departure coincided with the advent of another more exalted personage in the dining room. It was Abdul Haroon himself, the proprietor and maître d'hotel of the Golden Crescent. He billowed in past the bar, resplendent in a red silk tunic which may or may not have resembled some mode of Pakistani national dress, and sailed towards the Saint's table like a runaway balloon on a weakening wind.

He was, as if to advertise the bountiful nourishment he could offer, fat. His face was as nearly a perfect circle as a human countenance can be, and within it were the two nearly perfect circles of the lenses of his steel-rimmed spectacles. The roundness of his face was emphasised by the fact that before the onslaughts of time his hair had withdrawn from the area of his brow to form a secondary line of defence farther back on his scalp. His hair itself was as black as tar and glistened as if it had been copiously anointed with the same ghee in which its owner's cook fried the chopped lamb.

There was a babyish look built into Abdul Haroon's pliant features, and his voice had what promised to be a permanently youthful tone and lilt.

"Greetings, Mr Simon Templar, greetings!" he declaimed, parting the air between him and his customer with a pair of beringed hands. "You do me honour. I am so sorry we have not seen you in such a long time."

The Saint's reputation had reached a point where he no longer stood much chance of remaining incognito anywhere in London, and he had to comfort himself over that loss of the advantages of anonymity with the knowledge that restaurant service was often considerably better when the Saint was on the receiving end than it might have been for some less distinguished, or less notorious patron. Abdul Haroon, as soon as he had found out who Simon was during one of his first visits, had asked him for a large signed portrait-photograph which would be hung in a prominent spot on the dining-room wall, but Simon had gently declined the invitation.

"And I'm sorry I haven't been here," he told Abdul. "I'd be happy to run through the whole menu twice a month if I could find the time."

Abdul rotated with pleasure and glanced around hopefully to see if there were any other patrons within earshot. Unhappily, there were still no other patrons at all, but he failed to let that dampen his good spirits—good spirits which the Saint found remarkable considering the unwholesome circumstances in which Abdul had just lost one of his employees.

Mahmud brought Simon's Peter Dawson and retreated quickly.

"You are too kind, too kind!" the rotund restaurateur declaimed. "If all customers were as appreciative as yourself it would be enough to inspire even the wretched charlatans who wheedle their way into my employment pretending to be cooks."

It was one of Abdul's customs to imply that all the creatures of the earth were allied in the common cause of bringing about his financial, physical, and mental ruin. His employees, finding him otherwise kind, considerate, and even relatively generous, learned to tolerate his lamentations with resigned good humour, knowing that the more pleased he was the more likely he was to implore the heavens to witness the imminence of his downfall.

Simon tried to catch Abdul's eyes behind the glint of his round-lensed spectacles.

"You have staff problems?" he asked pointedly.

"Always, always," Abdul mourned. Now he was like a balloon going through a minor deflation. "They come and they go. I teach them to prepare and serve foods worthy of paradise and they take jobs as auto mechanics—or run away to trade the secrets they have learned from me for a job in some giant overdecorated mess-hall for American tourists where the tips are bigger and the management is not on the verge of bankruptcy . . ."

Abdul, being a balloon, seemed never to run short on his air supply, but the Saint interrupted him.

"According to this newspaper, all your ex-staff aren't so lucky."

For a moment Abdul looked as if he were going to ignore the Saint's allusion altogether and go right on babbling about his own endless tribulations. But unlike his waiter, Mahmud, Abdul had not been endowed by nature with the makings of a poker face. His features were too soft. They melted and welled into an expression of still more intense distress. His ring-laden hands clung to one another for support.

"Horrible, horrible!" he whispered.

"It is," Simon responded. "I had the impression for a minute that you hadn't heard about it yet."

"Oh, yes," Abdul moaned. He shifted his eyes first to one side and then the other, this time to make sure there were no other customers in the room. "It is a tragedy. It is in all the ruddy papers. It will ruin me!"

"It certainly ruined Ali," Simon said. "Have you seen this article?"

He opened the paper to the Tam Rowan story on page three, but in the meantime Abdul's original distress had burgeoned into full-blown fear.

"I have not," he answered hoarsely. "I don't want to. If a man who works for me gets himself involved with criminals it is none of my affair! Now . . . I'm sorry, but you must excuse me. I . . . I'm needed in the kitchen."

Abdul all but ran for cover and was replaced by Mahmud with a menu. Mahmud was no more communicative than before.

"Thank you," he intoned professionally, and turned to leave, but the Saint called him back.

"Mahmud," he asked with soft insistence, "who is it you're afraid of—me, the police, or the inventive chaps who killed your friend?"

Mahmud's eyes were now as evasive as Abdul's had been.

"He was not my friend," he announced curtly. "He was not a man to make friends. He never talked about himself, and I never saw him except here."

"An unsociable type," Simon mused, "but was that enough reason to kill him?"

Mahmud lost his aplomb for the first time.

"Kill him?" he exclaimed in a shocked whisper. "You cannot be suggesting that I or anyone here killed him!"

"I didn't intend to suggest anything," Simon answered. "I could hardly know, could I? You and your associates don't seem to talk any more about yourselves than you say Ali did."

Mahmud completed a carefully controlled deep breath.

"We are here to serve the customers," he said stiffly.

The Saint took a deep breath of his own. He realised that he had been overoptimistic to imagine that Abdul Haroon or one of his employees would take the first opportunity to blurt out their secret troubles to his sympathetic ear, the way bullied townspeople do in Western movies as soon as the hero lopes into town. Apparently the fear of these Pakistanis was so overpowering that they were afraid even to admit that they had anything to fear. With Ali's grisly example fresh in their minds, their attitude was not really surprising. It at least confirmed that Ali's fate was not the handiwork of a couple of madmen who had chosen their victim more or less at random. The force that had twisted out Ali's life had also threatened his co-workers.

"Mahmud," the Saint said earnestly, "I am not here just to eat, and I'm certainly not here out of idle curiosity." He leaned forward and rested his elbows on the newspaper and looked at Mahmud with disconcerting blue eyes. A little bluff seemed necessary to lubricate the wheels of confession. "I happen to know that Ali was not eliminated by a jealous husband or somebody who didn't like the way he served the sambuls. He was killed because he got in the way of the racketeers who're picking the bones of illegal immigrants from Pakistan and India after they get into this country. He was killed in the picturesque way he was so that other rebellious souls would feel a little less enthusiastic about shouting their complaints from the rooftops—or even whispering them to nosy characters like me. I don't think I can put it any more clearly than that, and I don't think I need to. My almost infallible intuition tells me that you're already several chapters ahead of me."

Mahmud was as unmoved as the Taj Mahal would have been by a light breeze.

"I am sorry, sir," he said.

"So am I, but I suggest you talk this over with your boss in the back room and see if you can't come up with something a little more helpful than cold sweat." He handed back the menu unopened. "And while you're back there, please order me some samosas, lamb curry, pilau rice, dhal, and all the sambuls you can crowd on the table."

"Thank you, sir." Simon had to admire the inappropriately arctic tones in which Mahmud uttered his next words. "And how would you like the curry, sir? Mild, medium, or hot?"

"Very hot."

"Thank you, sir."

The Saint was left alone with his drink and his newspaper for just a few seconds. At the end of that brief interval, the street door opened and the Golden Crescent's second customer of the early evening walked in, looked around, noted the Saint and the absence of waiters, and stood for a minute near the doorway as if wanting stubbornly to be greeted by people who were not there. He was a medium-weight tweedy man with sandy hair and moustache and ruddy cheeks. His face and the backward flow of his hair looked as if they had been sculpted to their present form by a strong headwind.

Simon would probably not have paid so much attention to the grey-suited man's appearance if he had not already decided that his newspaper contained no other fascinating journalistic revelations, and settled back against the comfortably padded backrest to sip his iced whisky while he waited for a chance to continue his own probing. If the new customer had not come in he would have had nothing to watch but the change of light on the walls and the passage of cars in the street outside. Now he could observe Civilized Man of the insecurely pretentious sort attempting to assert his authority in a near vacuum.

"Wonderful service around here," the newcomer remarked loudly.

"I understand they've had staff problems," Simon said.

The man had moved over near him, looking down the passageway which led to the kitchen.

"Staff shortage?" he said. "I can't understand why, with these Indian chaps pouring into the country like water into a torpedoed ship." He stationed himself by a table nearby, refusing to sit down until he was properly greeted. "Mind," he added with a guilty glance over his shoulder as if for the Thought Police of the Egalitarian State, "I've nothing against them as such, but we hardly need more people, do we?"

"We need less of some and more of others," the Saint responded. He motioned indicatively with his glass. "If you want to stake a claim on that table I'll be your witness."

The other man lost some of his stiffness, gave a single-shot snorting laugh, and sat down.

"I mean, dammit, I can't believe they've got a personnel problem. I should think there'd be eight men for every job. That's what it's coming to anyway, isn't it? People breeding like rabbits everywhere. Be living ten to a room and eating nothing but seaweed in fifty years, won't we?"

"I won't," said Simon, "but you have a point."

"Well, I won't either. I had my day, back when we still ruled the waves, or a good many of them. It's the next generation that's going to choke on these policies. I've spent some time out in India, and it's damned obvious why those chaps want to get out and come here, especially since we turned tail and ran. It's not so damned obvious why the Government welcomes 'em here with open arms. But then it's not obvious why the Government does anything, unless it's to appease all the loud mouths and empty pockets in the United Nations."

"That's as good a guess as I've heard," Simon agreed. "But you sound even more bitter than most of us."

"I've got reason to be. I was professional Navy, did what I could around Malta and Cyprus and a few other holiday spots during the war. And now . . ."

He shrugged.

"Caught in the cutbacks?" Simon asked.

"Cutbacks isn't the word for it," the red-faced man said. "Massacre, I'd call it. If you want to drive a ship and you're good at it, you've still got just a one in four chance of moving up, and after that it's four-to-one against you again." He sat back and expelled air through puffed cheeks. "So, I'm a pensioner. Fifteen quid a week for the rest of my life." He said it like a prisoner sharing the details of his sentence. "Nothing much to look forward to but sitting out my old age in Hove with a lot of other cast-offs while the country sinks under sheer weight of foreigners and the Government distributes largesse to everybody who can work up enough steam to reproduce." He suddenly looked at Simon. "Have you been to India?"

"Yes, but only as a private citizen."

"Like it?"

"I like the food," Simon said temperately. "And it seems as if you do, too."

"Right. Burns the soot out of the system. I've seen men half dead of dysentery cured with a good hot curry." He peered around the unstaffed room with renewed irritation. "Looks as if we'll be half dead with starvation before we get any." He looked back at Simon. "What do you think of this immigration business?"

The Saint pondered the question for a few seconds, but it was a question destined to fade unanswered into nothingness along with the last dying luminescence of the evening on the walls of the buildings opposite.

In the back room of the restaurant, a man screamed.

4

The Saint came to his feet, while his neighbour sat frozen bolt upright in his chair, staring towards the passageway that led past the bar. His once garrulous lips were petrified and pale, and he did not even break his sphynx-like pose when Simon strode away towards the rear of the dining room. Just after he reached the narrow hall beside the bar his way was blocked by Abdul Haroon, who came tottering in from the kitchen area with a handkerchief pressed to the side of his face.

"No reason for alarm or upset, ladies and gentlemen!" he burbled hysterically towards a mythical audience in the dining room. "A small accident in the kitchen. Everything will be immediately all right!"

The long agonised shriek that had reached the Saint's ears had been no result of a finger sliced along with the onions or a cheek spattered with hot fat.

"I'll have a look," he told Abdul. "I've got a Boy Scout badge in domestic first aid."

Abdul continued to interpose his bulk between Simon and the mysteries of the scullery, where a hurried scuffling of feet implied that the fun and games were not completely over yet.

"Sorry, Mr Haroon, but I'm afraid I'll have to violate the regulations. You're not hurt, are you?"

"No," Abdul said dazedly.

"Then I'd better go and see who is hurt. Pardon me."

Simon grasped Abdul's round shoulders firmly and simply moved him aside. As he hurried down the short passage he heard the proprietor lumbering ponderously to catch up with him.

The kitchen of the Golden Crescent was amazingly small and cramped, reminiscent of the interior of an early-model U-boat. There was no sign of a boiler explosion or the collapse of a stove. One panic-stricken cook had propped himself cataleptically against the greasy refrigerator and was staring at the open door of the storage pantry. The other cook and a waiter whose name Simon did not know were in that doorway ineffectually moving forward and backwards like two particles trapped in a fluctuating magnetic field.

Beyond their legs the Saint could see someone writhing on the floor of the storage pantry. Reaching the two frightened and hesitant men who were blocking the way, Simon saw over their shoulders that the party on the floor was Mahmud, who had waited on him. Mahmud lay moaning, his eyes squeezed shut, his knees drawn up, his left hand clutching his right arm. As he twisted in pain his white jacket was blotched and smeared with grime from the wooden floor. There was no sign of blood.

The Saint took in the details of the scene in one second, scarcely pausing behind the men who were already there.

As he shoved his way past them they gibbered at one another and at him in an incomprehensible amalgam of English and their native dialects.

"What happened and who did it?" Simon snapped.

All he could make out from the ensuing linguistic detonation were the words, "Arm broken!"

He did not stop beside Mahmud any longer than he had stopped behind the other two men.

"Call a doctor!" he threw over his shoulder.

If he had waited to inspect Mahmud or question the incoherent witnesses, anybody who had made the assault and fled could be putting half the West End between himself and the scene of his crime. There were only two doors to the Golden Crescent, the front and the back, and nobody had left through the front. Simon hurried on through the narrow room, rich with the smells of the condiments on its shelves, and out of the back door into the alley where he had seen the van parked not long before. There was no van and nobody in the semi-darkness of the alley now, no Indian Gulliver with Lilliputian helper.

The Saint paused for an instant, looking both ways to be doubly sure the alley was free of any possible danger, and then he ran to the corner and the sidewalk where he had passed on his way to the restaurant. He was sure that he saw the van which conveyed the purveyors of Indian foodstuffs losing itself in the traffic almost a block away. A recollection of the giant delivery man glowed to brief vividness in his mind, but knowing that he had no chance of identifying the mayhem merchant, whoever he was and whether he was in the van or not, Simon retraced his steps to the back door of the restaurant.

In the small storeroom Mahmud still lay on the floor, but Abdul Haroon and the uninjured waiter were kneeling beside him. Mahmud's eyes were open now, and though his face was tense with pain he was completely conscious.

He turned his head fearfully to see who had come in the door, but tended to relax again when he saw that it was the Saint. Abdul looked more confused than his prostrate employee.

"Where did you go?" he asked Simon.

"To see if I could catch whoever did whatever's been done," said the Saint matter-of-factly. "I didn't."

He was standing beside Abdul now.

"His arm is broken," the owner of the Golden Crescent told him.

Mahmud looked up at the Saint almost pleadingly.

"It was an accident," he said.

Simon narrowed his eyes with disbelief.

"An accident?" he asked. "I'm sorry to have to take an ironic attitude in a time of personal tragedy for you, my friend, but what did you do—catch your arm in an egg-beater?"

"He slipped," the other waiter said vaguely.

"A box fell," added one of the cooks from the doorway for good measure.

The Saint knelt next to Abdul and Mahmud.

"I'd have been more likely to conclude that one of your competitors was trying to do you out of your waiters the hard way," he averred.

He reached to touch Mahmud's limp arm, but the injured man winced in agony as Simon put pressure on it, and tried to shrink away.

Haroon told one of the cooks to call for a taxi to pull into the alley, and the man scuttled out.

"We will take him to a doctor," Haroon explained to Simon. "We know one near here."

"At the rate you're going, you might as well hire one to stay in residence," the Saint said. He stood up suddenly, stepped back, and faced the whole group. "Now let's try to bring a little realism to this Never-Never Land. As far as I can tell through all the polite fog, you've got every intention of sitting tight while the bad guys walk all over you with king-sized boots. There's not much point in being discreet if you end up like Mahmud here."

There was an embarrassed and very deep silence. Abdul finally spoke.

"It would be worse to end up like Ali," he said in a voice that was almost a whisper.

The mere fact that he had found the courage to refer to Ali gave Simon hope.

"I don't expect anybody to sign a complaint," he said, "but I'm not the police so there's no need to sign anything. I think Mr Haroon at least has an idea of how I work. Just give me a hint—or get in touch with me later if you won't talk in front of other people."

He stopped and waited, feeling slightly ridiculous as another long silence followed. Abdul got to his feet next to Simon and avoided looking at him.

"But it was only an accident," he muttered.

Simon looked around at his otherwise mute audience in exasperation. Before he could think of anything appropriately galvanising to say, the cook who had taken off came running back in.

"Taxi here!" he announced.

Behind him, through the open door, Simon could see the lights of the black taxi in the alley.

"Help me," Mahmud groaned.

They lifted him carefully to his feet, and he was able to walk very slowly out to the car, supported by Abdul and one of the cooks. Abdul told his last operational waiter and his second cook to get back on the job before his reputation was so besmirched that he would be reduced in this, his intolerable old age, to hawking chestnuts in Piccadilly Circus.

Simon saw Mahmud safely into the taxi. The cook looked questioningly at Abdul.

"Yes, go with him, go with him!" the restaurant-owner cried in despair, flapping the cook into the automobile with the backs of both hands. "I am already destroyed. What does it matter—one cook, two cooks, no cook? I am utterly and completely undone!"

His whole body sagged as the cook scrambled into the taxi with the injured man and the cab pulled away. With a Lear-like expression of total despair he faced the Saint for an instant and then walked slowly towards the open door of the Golden Crescent. Simon reached out and closed it before Abdul could step inside. The sky was almost completely dark now, and there were no artificial lights in the alley itself. Abdul's eyes, as they met the Saint's at close range, were large with fear, reflecting the moving illuminations of the street at the corner.

"I must . . . see to my customers," he said desperately.

As he pushed towards the door Simon barred his way with an outstretched arm so efficiently strong that it would have taken ten Abduls to move it.

"I'm one of your customers," the Saint said, "and I'm always right." He relaxed a little as Abdul stopped trying to push past him. "Besides, I have priority. I was the first one here tonight and I still haven't been waited on, and I'm getting a little tired of waiting in general."

Abdul made a futile effort to misinterpret.

"I am sorry, Mr Templar, but you understand . . . As soon as possible you will have your dinner."

Simon leaned back against the closed door and folded his arms, regarding Abdul in the darkness as a circus trainer might regard a recalcitrant seal.

"Let's stop playing patty cake, shall we? I'm embarrassed enough for myself without having to be embarrassed for you."

"Embarrassed?" Abdul asked.

"Yes, embarrassed. I'm a natural-born anarchist, and if there's one thing I'd just as soon step on as look at it's a do-gooder who tries to help people who don't want his help. But that's what you're making me feel like."

Abdul shifted his feet miserably.

"I'm sorry."

Simon hesitated thoughtfully.

"I'm beginning to think you people enjoy being bashed."

Abdul did not say anything.

"We're obviously alone out here," the Saint argued. "Nobody can hear us. I feel like dropping the whole subject and sticking to Italian restaurants from now on, but I hate to let something go once I've got a hold on it. So why don't you at least give me a lead?"

Abdul still did not say anything.

"What about King Kong and his pint-sized playmate who were toting groceries through this very door at about the time Mahmud had his accident? They must have seen it . . . or done it."

He could sense the electric tension that suddenly stiffened Abdul's body, and he could see the confused surprise on the fat man's face.

"How did you know they were here?" Abdul croaked.

"I was admiring them on my way in."

"They . . ." Abdul stopped and shrugged. "They had left, of course, or they would have stayed . . . to help after the accident."

Simon took in a deep breath and blew it tiredly out again.

"Oh, Mr Haroon, you are very good at running a restaurant but very bad at lying. I'll try once more: would you just give me the name of the driver of that van and the address of Supreme Imports?"

Abdul, sensing reprieve in the wind, spoke more vehemently.

"I don't know the driver's name. There is no need to. And Supreme Imports . . ." He shrugged. "I do not happen to know their address since their salesman called on me here originally and all our business has been done here since then."

Simon saw no reason to continue wasting his time. He stepped away from the door and opened it.

"After you, then. I've enjoyed our talk. It's nice to meet a man without a care in the world."

Abdul smiled wanly and dabbed his handkerchief against his perspiring fat cheeks.

"After you, Mr Templar," he said in a loud voice. "It is very good of you to be so concerned about poor Mahmud."

Simon went disgustedly back through the kitchen, where his very existence was conscientiously ignored and down the hallway to his table. His red-cheeked acquaintance who had once ruled the waves had disappeared, perhaps understandably, but several more innocent diners had taken other places in the room. The other waiter, soon reinforced by Abdul's frenetic help, was running from errand to errand in a valiant effort to please them. Almost as soon as the Saint sat down his food was served, but he had scarcely any real appetite left. Like a mathematician with a teasing problem in his head, he found it hard to think of anything but the challenge towards which he had set his course when he had entered the Golden Crescent in the first place. Briefly, out of disgust with the terror-stricken reticence of Abdul and his staff, he had felt like dropping the whole tentative project and leaving them to sweat out their own problems, but on reflection the silence of the Pakistanis seemed more a challenge than their co-operation would have been. And then there was that muttonchop-whiskered Goliath and his pipsqueak partner . . . and that daring reporter, Mr Tam Rowan . . . all in all, ingredients which properly blended might provide as much excitement as the Saint had enjoyed in a long long while.

By the time he had finished his dinner Simon had no more thoughts of quitting left in his head. His mind was simmering with plans and possibilities, and he was as eager as a hound for the chase.

As if in reward for his determination, there was a little surprise waiting for him when he opened the folded bill which Abdul himself left on his table. A hasty hand had pencilled five words in the margin which had nothing to do with the menu:

Don't! They would kill anybody.

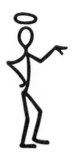

CHAPTER TWO:

HOW THE SAINT MET TAM ROWAN AND THEY HEARD OF A RENDEZVOUS

1

The Saint placed a five-pound note—one pound for each word of the pencil-scribbled warning—on the small tray with his dinner bill, and Abdul Haroon immediately scooted over from the centre of the room and confiscated it.

"Thank you, sir! Thank you very much! One moment for the change . . ."

"Give it to Mahmud," Simon said, getting to his feet. "He won't be picking up many tips for a few weeks."

He searched the restaurant-owner's round perspiring face for some trace of admission that it was Abdul himself who had written the note, but he met only an impenetrable determinedly smiling mask.

"You are most kind," Abdul said.

He was bowing the Saint to the door. The bill and the five-pound note had already disappeared into his pocket.

"And you are very good about looking after your customers," Simon rejoined.

"I must try to look after them well," Abdul said gloomily. "They are few enough!"

Even as the Saint nodded good-night just before stepping into the street Abdul's expression betrayed nothing. He bowed again with elaborate politeness and held the door open. Simon left without another word, deciding to accept the remembered message for what it was worth and not press matters any further at the Golden Crescent.

But just what was the warning worth? When he was alone on the sidewalk outside the restaurant he thought it over briefly. There had been no information in it, nothing he could draw any help from. He was still just where he had been after Mahmud's implausible accident. He had a newspaper story bylined by a man who claimed to know more about the illegal immigration racket than he apparently dared to reveal, and he had in his head the name of a wholesale food-distribution company whose employees had shown conspicuous alacrity in getting on to their next job after doing whatever they had done at the Golden Crescent that evening.

Simon stood on the street corner and watched the cars and taxis and evening crowds hurrying by, regretting that he had not memorized the delivery van's licence. But at the time he had noticed the truck there had been no reason to believe he would ever need to know its number.

There was a telephone outside a pub not far down the street. The Saint walked down to it, stepped into the tobacco-acrid atmosphere of the red kiosk, and swivelled the "S" volume of the directory up so he could have a look at it. He soon satisfied himself, without any great astonishment, that there was no Supreme Imports Ltd. in the London area—or at least that Supreme Imports (whatever it might be they imported) did not feel the need of a listed telephone in the transaction of their business. To make sure, he dialled directory inquiries, asked if Supreme Imports had a number, and received the expected negative answer.

Without leaving the telephone booth the Saint glanced at his wristwatch. It was still early in the evening, but any respectable importing company would have closed its doors by now anyway—and those which specialized in not quite so respectable imports were not likely to make wassail for the stranger at their gates at any hour. Simon put the "S" volume of the directory back to bed and opened the one that contained "R."

There were half a column of "Rowans" inhabiting London, but of that illustrious clan only one, fortunately, possessed the first name of "Tam." He also, fortunately, maintained a telephone, and he dwelt at Belsize Square.

The existence of Mr Rowan's telephone was of use to Simon mainly as a guide to the address. He had had enough of the silent treatment at the Golden Crescent. He was not going to risk giving Rowan the same easy way out by making his approach over the phone. He would beard the star reporter in his own lair.

The theatre crowds were in their playhouses by now, and the restaurant rush had not yet begun, so the streets in Simon's vicinity were swarming with whole schools of unoccupied taxis. He commandeered one and was soon carried out of the whirlpool of the Piccadilly Circus-Leicester Square area into the more smoothly flowing streams farther north.

The street where he eventually stopped might have been two hundred miles in space or fifty years back in time from the thronged centre of London he had left behind just a few minutes before. Around Belsize Square Simon's departing taxi was the only moving vehicle. Not even one solitary human being strolled the lamplit sidewalks. The trees were big, and so were the quiet houses—three- and four-storey buildings shoulder to shoulder, with hedged gardens in front. Each garden, it seemed, was the property of a cat, and each cat Simon passed (he had gotten out of the taxi some distance from his destination so as not to advertise his arrival) was constructed on the same ample scale as the trees and the houses. They were great fat lazy trusting beasts ready to roll over on the sidewalk for a stomach rub by any human who happened to wander past their respective territories.

Simon obliged several friendly felines with a scratch and a pat, and thought that he rather admired Tam Rowan for choosing a neighbourhood so rich in animals, old trees, and nostalgia. It was not exactly the sort of section he would have expected an ambitious journalist to roost in—especially a journalist who got his name printed above lavish articles which were mentioned on the front page of his newspaper.

Rowan's address led the Saint up a short walk presided over by a ginger cat too sluggish even to watch him go by. Simon mounted the cement stairs at the end of the walk, which brought him to a heavy oak door, the only part of the three-storey house which was not painted white. To the right of the door was a battery of six bell-buttons variously stained with use according to the popularity of their owners. Identifying cards, ranging from the finest engraved script to ballpoint longhand on a piece of wrapping-paper, were inserted in the slots next to the push-buttons.

The Saint passed over Mr and Mrs Beasley, grimaced at Laverne Larousse, Private Tutor, and was gratified to learn that his own Tam Rowan lived in flat number 4.

The oak door of the house was not locked, so Simon opened it and walked into the dark hall. There was a pleasant smell of chocolate cake baking, and the muted sound of a television set or radio. The only light in the entrance hall came from under the door of one of the flats. Simon found the electric switch just inside the main entrance, wondering if perhaps the landlord had removed the bulbs from the public corridors for reasons of economy. But an overhead light came on at a flick of his finger and he could see his way up the broad heavily bannistered stairway to the next floor.

The sound of the loudspeaker which he had heard on the ground floor became louder as he climbed the neatly carpeted, slightly creaking stairs. Some species of chaos comparable to a Roman combat between Nubian dwarves and crazed baboons seemed—judging from the auditory indications—to be taking place before a screaming audience of thousands. Simon hoped fervently that the cacophony was not issuing from apartment number 4, but it was.

The varnished door with its brass numeral was closed firmly, but the sounds of slaughter came clearly from within by way of a crevice next to the floor. Simon listened for a few seconds and then knocked. There was no response. During a lull in the roaring he knocked again, this time more firmly, and a few seconds later he heard a woman's voice from just inside, as if she had her mouth pressed almost directly against the door.

"Who is it?" she asked.

"I'd like to see Mr Tam Rowan," Simon said.

"Who are you?" the female voice enquired with something close to outright hostility.

"Not the big bad wolf," Simon told her. "If you'll open the door you'll be reassured by my clean-cut and well-groomed appearance."

There was a pause, and then a key turned in the lock on the other side of the door. The Saint felt that the wariness of the key-turner was completely understandable, considering that Reporter Rowan had been threatened with death by people who had already shown themselves quite capable of carrying out such threats. He was a little surprised, in fact, that he was being let in after such a short period of persuasion. And then, as the door opened three inches, he realised that he had another barrier to get past: there was a chain-lock preventing the door from being pushed any farther.

A pair of bright turquoise eyes appeared cautiously above the chain, and as little else of a lightly freckled face as the girl could show.

"What do you want?" she asked.

"I've told you. I want to see the journalist of the house."

"What for?" she asked unblinkingly.

"I sell submarines," said Simon.

"Very funny."

"Not very," the Saint said. "I also bargain for information, and I enjoy meeting people who share my interests—in things like smuggled immigrants. Why don't you let me in so we can swap stories without all the neighbours getting an earful."

"Because I don't know who you are and I don't trust you," she said bluntly.

"My name is Simon Templar, and those who tread the paths of righteousness can trust me from here to the moon. Does that answer your questions?"

Her cold blue-green eyes narrowed as she looked him up and down and scrutinized his face.

"You say you're Simon Templar . . . the Saint?" she asked.

"Bingo," he said. "The very man."

She squinted at his face again.

"I really think you are."

"I'd be awfully disappointed to find out I wasn't," he replied. "Think of it: getting somebody else's laundry all these years. And who are you—a Rowan or something else?"

"I am the Rowan," she said.

"Tam Rowan of crime-busting fame?" he asked with a lift of his brows.

"Right."

"Shades of Amos Klein," said the Saint.

2

"What?" she said blankly.

"She was another lad who turned out not to be a lad," Simon explained. "I wish you emancipated females would retain some identifying characteristics in your names."

"It's too dangerous," she said. If there was any relaxation in her tone it was the relaxation of a lion trainer between acts. "Strange men find out a woman is living alone and knock on her door at night."

"Well, now that it's happened what are you going to do about it?" he asked her.

"I'm going to let you in because I know you are the Saint because now I remember I've seen your picture—but if you try to get close to me I'll yell so loud they'll have to replace every crystal chandelier in this woodworm palace."

"I'll try to control any romantic impulses and keep my distance," Simon said with exaggerated regret.

She slipped the chain free and opened the door, standing well back as he stepped into the room. Her bearing, if not her shape, reminded him of a drill sergeant looking over new recruits.

"Now you go to the middle of the room while I close the door," she instructed him in a voice whose toughness matched her wary stance.

Simon strolled to the centre of the flat. The sitting room was simply but well furnished, mostly in gold and green, with a well-stocked bookshelf and a Breughel winter landscape above the fireplace. He decided he liked the person who lived there. There was a lack of show or of self-conscious nonchalance, and a feeling of honest use.

"Is this all right?" he asked, indicating the portion of carpet he was occupying.

She nodded as she closed the door. One of her hands remained, as if by a series of casual accidents in her movements, behind her.

"I don't know if it's more dangerous to lock myself in here with you or to leave it open and take a chance on somebody else barging in," she said without a smile.

She was reasonably pretty, but not beautiful. Her healthy broad-cheeked face had too much of a Nordic peasant quality for the latter adjective. Her nose was pertly small, and combined with the crescent lilt of her mouth it gave her a built-in saucy look. Her light hair was cut short and fell with a defiant jaggedness around her ears and forehead. She wore a plain blouse that she filled rather nicely, blue jeans, and no shoes.

Simon faced her easily, lean and dark, sizing her up with the disconcerting directness of his gaze.

"Who else are we expecting?" he asked.

She had locked the door and come a short distance towards him.

"Some chums who've promised to slice me up in little pieces if I don't stop immortalising them in print," she said.

"Then that wasn't just artistic licence for spicing-up your story."

"Of course not," she said curtly. "You read the story, in the paper tonight? Is that why you're here?"

"Mainly. I could discuss the whole thing more comfortably if you'd take that butcher's knife out from behind your back, though."

She flushed slightly, a reaction he was sure she detested, signalling that he had hit the mark.

"What knife?" she countered uselessly.

"Girls who turn red when rattled should never try to keep secrets," said Simon. "It's really rather foolish of you to think you're hiding anything."

She showed her concealed hand, and it did indeed contain a large kitchen knife.

"It may seem kinky to you," she said, "but at least I'm safe."

He smiled a little sadly.

"You really think so?"

Her eyes flashed and she stepped towards him, trying to give him a scare by poking the point of the knife to within a foot or so of his chest.

"Yes!" she said.

She never did know exactly what had happened just after her "yes." Instead of flinching away from the knife as she had expected, the Saint stepped aside and towards her with the fluid grace of a matador. She was not aware of what his hands were doing, but suddenly she was standing open-mouthed without her knife and he was holding it and regarding it as if it had been an interesting shell he had picked up on a beach.

"You really shouldn't play with things like this," he said gently. "It belongs in the kitchen, after all, along with grapefruit and women."

Her teeth were set with fury, and suddenly without a sound she exploded and grabbed for his knife hand. He effortlessly evaded the lunge and caught her hard up against him, pinning her strong upper arms against her ribs.

"You are a vicious bird, aren't you?" he chided.

"You're a pig!" she spat.

Wishing to get free, she managed to raise her left hand almost to the level of his face. Just in time he realised that she was consciously doing something with her thumb to the inner part of a massive golden ring on her fourth finger. As her hand flexed he tilted his head aside and pushed her wrist away from him with his free hand.

In that instant there was a barely audible fizzle, and an almost microscopic quantity of some gaseous vapour puffed feebly from the centre of the heavily wrought metal of the ring, most of it into the girl's own eyes.

"Curse!" she exploded.

Then she was coughing and squeezing her eyelids tightly shut, and tears were streaming down the freckled, milk-smooth skin of her cheeks.

Simon was supporting her rather than holding her against her will, and she was making no more effort to get away.

"What was that supposed to be?" he enquired kindly.

"Go ahead," she growled. "Kill me. Get it over with."

"That's a very tempting suggestion, but I need you too much—for the moment." He tossed the kitchen knife onto a sofa and lifted her left hand so that he could inspect the golden ring. "Is that Renaissance poison-squirter something you got out of a breakfast-food box?"

She rubbed her eyes with her free hand.

"It's a tear-gas ring," she answered sullenly. "Or at least it's supposed to be. It always worked when I was testing it."

"It seems like a terribly inefficient form of suicide," he said. "Something like trying to fold yourself to death in an ironing board. Most people find that shooting themselves with guns works pretty well."

One corner of her mouth switched in what suspiciously resembled the germination of a smile.

"I don't have a gun!" she snapped, killing the smile. "And if the damn thing had worked you'd have got the tear gas right in your face."

"And afterwards you'd have cracked me over the head with a table lamp?" he suggested.

"Preferably with a poker," she replied.

He let her go, and she stepped back rubbing her shoulder to convey the false impression that he had hurt it. In spite of the fiercely belligerent expression on her face he deduced that the war was over and that the next step was to define the conditions of peace.

"Well, love at first sight is dandy," he said, "but isn't it time we got on with more serious things? May I sit down?"

"Apparently I can't stop you."

He settled on to the sofa, flipped the long kitchen knife up into the air by its point, and caught it by its handle, all the while smiling at her in the most dazzlingly benign way imaginable.

"Well?" she asked, unimpressed.

"It's very nice to be here," he said. "It isn't every day I meet a fearless girl reporter. They should print your picture along with your articles."

"Why?"

"It would boost circulation, for one thing."

Once more a bit of sun threatened to break through her cloudy expression, but she fought it back and with mock symptoms of muscular anguish perched on the arm of an overstuffed chair opposite him. The pretence of pain struck him as a fascinating plea for sympathy beneath her granite outer layers.

"You may be the Saint," she said, "but I'll bet you're here spying for another newspaper, trying to nose in on all my research."

"Even you don't believe that," Simon responded casually. "Or else you're the wildest romantic since Richard Strauss. I'll tell you why I'm here: you're an expert on the immigrant-blackmail racket . . ." He stopped and nodded towards the television set, which had been on the periphery of his mind for some time. "And speaking of racket, couldn't we cut down the volume of that mayhem?"

"It's my telly and I'll play it as flaming loud as I please!" she retorted defiantly.

Simon sighed.

"I'm sure you will. I assume that an obnoxious pugnaciousness is a permanent part of your character?"

She got up and turned the volume of the television down and—even more unexpectedly—actually smiled.

"Impertinence is the word," she said. "I'm impertinent, because my face is impertinent. It's my nose and mouth." She prodded those features with her fingertips as if they were made of soft clay. "My nose is too small and my mouth is too big. They make me look impertinent even when I'm not, so I always used to get the blame for everything no matter what I did, so I reckoned if I were going to be accused of being impertinent anyway I might as well be impertinent."

"And pugnacious," the Saint insisted.

"Right." She gave him a silent tigerish snarl. "Now tell me what you're doing here before I gobble you up."

"Fine," said Simon. "Much to my subsequent regret I got interested in this immigration mess, read your article, and got involved. I came over here to see if you could help me. That's it."

"Just like that?" she asked sceptically. "Why are you interested? What got you involved? I thought you never got yourself into messes unless you were sure you could come out with a profit."

"The rewards of virtue have a way of not guaranteeing themselves until after you've committed yourself. I'm a speculator, you see, as well as a friend of the downtrodden. Now let's make this a two-way interview: since you obviously couldn't have known I was coming for a little *tetea-tete*, how come you were hiding behind the door with the welcome mat ready to toss over my head?"

The girl glanced at the blessedly silent television screen, where an almost perfectly cubical black-bearded man was bouncing a rubber boned African to and fro across the ring. Then she sat down.

"If you did read my article today you know the gang that killed that Pakistani last night threatened to cut me up if I said too much." She shrugged. "I thought you might be one of them."

"Now that you know different, how about telling me all about the rest of your singlehanded campaign against these thugs? I assume it's singlehanded."

"It is," she replied, "but I don't see why I should tell you anything. This is my living, friend, and even if you are the Saint how do I know you're not working for somebody who's not on my side?"

"As you grow to know and love me I'm sure you'll realise just how ludicrous that suggestion is. For one thing, why should anybody with my ill-gotten riches want to become an undercover agent for anybody—especially some tight-fisted scandal sheet?"

She shrugged uneasily.

"Why should anybody with the loot you're supposed to have stashed away want to do anything—except spend it?"

"Because life is action," Simon said. "Is that good enough for you?"

"No."

"You're hard to please."

"You're right. If I wasn't I'd still be juggling paper clips in some back office—and I wouldn't be single at the ripe old age of twenty-six."

"Getting worried about that?" Simon asked with a grin.

"No," she said with determined carelessness. "I didn't say I couldn't please, I said I was hard to please."

"Granted. Now, how about some kind of a deal between the two of us? You tell me what you know, I give you exclusive publishing rights to anything we find out, and I'll even undertake to keep you alive until the story's finished."

She was seriously considering his words now.

"It sounds like you get most of the benefits," she said after a few seconds. "I can keep myself alive and I've already got exclusive publishing rights on anything I find out."

"That's rather debatable," the Saint opined. "I wouldn't bet one moulting Bombay duck on your chances of being alive this time next week if you keep on the way you're going—and if I have to go into this thing without you I might have to ally myself with some rival of yours who's just as interested in a hot scoop as you are."

She sat up stiffly and stared at him in appalled outrage.

"Why, you . . . you . . ."

"Cad?" suggested Simon.

"Crook!" said the girl.

"Businessman," Simon amended. "Why fight it? We both stand to benefit."

She decided not to blast off, and settled into her chair cushions again.

"All right," she agreed reluctantly. "With one more condition: if we're going into this together we're really going into it together. You have to promise me you'll take me with you wherever you go and always tell me what's happening . . . especially that you'll take me everywhere you go and don't do anything without me."

"Sounds like an intriguing proposal," the Saint said.

His hostess flushed slightly, opened her mouth, and closed it again before she finally spoke.

"When there's a line to draw, I'll draw it," she said. "Do you agree?"

He hesitated just a few seconds before answering, then he raised his hands briefly in a gesture of acquiescence.

"Whither I go thou shalt go," he said. "It's a deal. And now, since we're going to become inseparable, may I ask what your intimates call you? 'Slugger?' 'Killer?'"

"Tammy," she said. "Any objections?"

"Not if I'm admitted to the club. So now let's get down to facts. Just how much do you really know about this immigration gang?"

"More than I had the nerve to print," she stated.

"I noticed you didn't name names. Do you know any?"

"Names?" she asked. "Yes, a couple. I don't know who's at the top of the whole thing, but I know who does the dirty work and I've got a pretty complete picture of the way the extortion side of the business operates."

"As part of our bargain, how about giving me the names of the thugs you do know?"

Tammy Rowan looked at him with a peculiar mysteriousness and then said something that rang an alarm through every fibre in his body.

"I'll do better than that: in just about ten seconds you can see one of them."

3

Tammy saw the Saint tense, and her turquoise eyes glinted with amusement. She pointed at the television screen.

"On there," she said. "Believe me, I haven't invited him up for supper."

She got out of her chair and turned up the volume of the television. One of the wrestling matches had ended and another was about to begin. The ring was empty except for the announcer, who was stepping into the centre with his microphone in hand. Tammy spoke before he did.

"The charming character you're about to see is the highest man on the totem pole that I know about," she said. "He's made himself a pile of money off the racket and you almost never see him wrestle anymore."

The crowd was cheering happily as a muscular sandy-haired young man with a face out of a toothpaste advertisement bounded into the wrestling ring.

"Clean-cut rat," Simon commented.

"That's not him," said the girl. "Here he comes."

The new arrival was accompanied down the aisle by a wave of jeers and boos which swelled to a crest as he climbed stolidly up on to the canvas in his corner. Even before he came from the aisle into the lights and turned so that the TV camera could catch his face Simon more than suspected who he was. Suddenly in close-up on the screen flashed the muttonchop-whiskered beady-eyed countenance of the huge man Simon had seen outside the Golden Crescent.

"We have a mutual acquaintance," he murmured with a quiet satisfaction.

She looked at him sharply. The announcer was introducing the sandy-haired wrestler, who drew cheers.

"You know him already?" she asked.

"The one with the weedy jowls? Yes. I haven't had the pleasure of a chat with him, but I saw him this evening for the first time."

The Saint and Tammy both paused and looked at the screen as the announcer pointed to the giant, silk-robed Pakistani.

"And in this corner, from London, weighing seventeen stone five, Kalki the Conqueror."

To coincide with his formal presentation to the unadoring public, Kalki the Conqueror stripped off his robe and raised both massive arms and flexed his muscles. The bombardment of the arena with eight tons of excruciatingly aromatic decayed eggs would have produced a more gleeful response in the crowd than did the unveiling of Kalki the Conqueror. Their collective howl rattled the loudspeaker, and several of their number ventured to stand up and shriek insults from the safety of the fourth, seventh, and tenth rows.

Kalki, in what was apparently a trademark combination of gestures, faced the crowd, and rubbed the bald top of his head vigorously with his left hand while he grimaced and roared at the mob.

"Popular chap," the Saint remarked.

"He might be funny if I didn't know what he did in his spare time," Tammy said. She forced her eyes from the spectacle on the television screen. "You saw him?" she asked. "When? Where?"

Simon told her about his arrival at the Golden Crescent—the van and the two men in the alley.

"Yes!" she interrupted eagerly. "That's him. And the little one with him, that was Shortwave!"

"Shortwave?" asked Simon.

"Yes. He's the other one whose name I know."

The wrestling match began with conventional circling and chary grappling, but Simon was more interested in his conversation with Tammy.

"What's the little one's real name?" he asked.

"How would I know his real name?" she asked impatiently. "My sources know people by what they're called, not by their birth certificates."

"So Kalki is just plain Kalki?"

"Right. That's his stage name, or whatever you call it, and that's how he's known."

"If he wrestles on TV he must have had to sign his real name on quite a few papers."

"Of course," she said with self-defensive impatience. "I could have found out his name. Anybody could have, and it would be just one more Pakistani-Moslem name. I'm interested in what he does, not in what his middle initial is." She leaned suddenly towards a side table and snatched a pack of cigarettes. She never did anything slowly. "Smoke?" she asked.

Simon shook his head and she lit one and left it between her lips as she talked.

"Of course I was going to find out his name," she said. "And Shortwave's, too, but I haven't been on this story as long as that article of mine today might imply. I haven't had time yet to go combing through other people's files, and I don't think I'll find out anything very useful when I do."

The Saint was watching the wrestling match as he listened to Tammy. Like other such displays it showed every symptom of being a preplanned ham performance which would be seen by the relatively sophisticated as a sadistically spiced athletic exhibition and by the dull-witted as an horrific battle between pure good and pure evil.

Kalki the Conqueror was, of course, pure evil. While his wholesome opponent remained calm in adversity, patient with every provocation, and obedient to the referee's commands, Kalki brutally raked his foe's neck over the ropes, twisted his ears, hit him in the lumbar region with his fist, tried to smother him by lying on his face, and indulged in a multitude of other illegal atrocities. But even the most minute successful use of force on Cleancut's part was enough to throw Kalki into titanic tantrums of lunatic rage.

The crowd adored hating him, and when suddenly Robin Goodfellow appeared to lose his temper and grabbed Kalki by his grandiose side-whiskers and hurled him over the ropes and out of the ring, the plebs went wild with delight. One righteous but emotional lady leapt from her seat and indignantly smote Kalki about the back and shoulders with her handbag as he crawled back onto the platform.

"You were going to tackle that with your 007 gas ring?" Simon asked, as the giant roared and shook his mighty fists at the audience.

"He's all hot air," Tammy said contemptuously. "Anyway, I knew he was on television tonight."

"Three hundred pounds of hot air is a lot of hot air," the Saint said. "A couple of hours ago I saw what it could do to a man's right arm."

She turned her head to look at him.

"How? What do you mean?"

"I didn't finish telling you what happened after I saw Kalki and his pal outside the restaurant this evening. Do you know anything about a waiter at the Golden Crescent named Mahmud?"

"No," said Tammy.

She got out of her chair and turned off the TV set, at the same time keeping her eyes intently on Simon as he went on with his story.

"Apparently he incurred the displeasure of the gang because one minute he was serving me a Peter Dawson and the next minute he was lying in the back room of the restaurant with a broken arm."

"Good grief!" Tammy exclaimed, and grabbed for the telephone at the end of the sofa.

"What are you doing?"

"Calling my paper, of course. You haven't told anybody else, have you?"

Simon jumped up and clamped his hand over the telephone dial before she could spin it more than once.

"No, I haven't," he said, "and you're not telling anybody, either."

She was aghast.

"Why not? They killed one man last night and broke another one's arm this evening. That's news, boyo!"

"I'm sure that with big enough headlines it could be made to look like news, but if you implied that Mahmud had run into anything more malignant than an unbalanced crate of beans you'd be letting yourself in for a lawsuit."

Tammy gave up her efforts to pry the phone from the Saint's immovable grasp.

"Who'd sue me?" she asked. "I'd only be reporting what happened."

Simon lifted his hand from the telephone.

"If you think that a waiter getting his arm fractured by a crate of beans falling off a shelf is news, go right ahead and call it in."

"You're kidding me. What really happened?"

"What really happened, I'm sure, is just what you think happened. But the waiter and the other lads from the scullery ain't seen nothing. They're as chatty as mourners at a Mafia funeral. And Kalki the Purveyor had scooted out the back of the storeroom and was well on his way to metamorphosing into Kalki the Conqueror by the time I got on to the scene."

The girl flopped back into her chair.

"Curse!" she said. "That's just what I've run into every time I think I'm getting somewhere on this thing. I wish . . ."

Whether in express-delivery answer to her wish or not, there were three cautious knocks at her door.

"Gad," she whispered. "Who could that be? You didn't bring any friends, did you?"

Simon shook his head. Both he and Tammy were on their feet.

"Maybe it's the little delegation you were expecting when I walked in," he suggested. "Ask who it is."

He stood aside while she leaned close to the door.

"Who's there?" she called.

"A friend," came frightened, foreign-accented words from the other side, "please, let me in quickly!"

Simon recognized the voice.

"Let him in," he murmured. "Keep well back, and I'll be right here to make sure nothing goes wrong."

Tammy looked at him searchingly, bit her lower lip, and turned the handle of the door.

There, pressed against the door frame like a sheep huddling for shelter against a blizzard, was Mahmud with his arm in a sling. He slipped inside with an anxious glance over his shoulder. Then he saw Simon and reacted first with sharp surprise and then with relief.

"Mr Templar!" was all he seemed able to gasp for the moment.

Tammy locked the door and stood away.

"I thought you two hadn't met," Simon said.

"We haven't," she answered. "Is this . . ."

"Mahmud," Simon confirmed. "I'm afraid I don't know the last name."

"Dehlavi," the Pakistani said. "Mahmud Dehlavi." His forehead was glistening with sweat and he was hugging his wounded arm close against him. "I came to see madame to tell . . . to tell things I know, because she writes in the paper."

"Sit down here," Tammy said, pushing a chair towards him. "You shouldn't be running around like that."

Mahmud Dehlavi lowered himself gingerly into the chair, clutching Simon's arm with his left hand for support.

"Did the doctor fix you up all right?" Simon asked. "Is it badly broken?"

Mahmud looked grimly at his white-swathed right arm, which was now in splints.

"It is fractured," he said, "but the bone was not separated."

"Still, that's a pretty fair job for a wooden crate to do," the Saint said without a trace of levity.

The slender Pakistani's dark eyes glowed like coals under a sudden blast of air.

"Mr Templar, Miss Rowan, can I trust you?" he asked.

"Of course," Tammy said.

She had settled on a chair facing her new guest. Simon still stood, looking down on both of them.

"You can trust us to do what's right, if that's what you mean," he stipulated.

"I must trust you," the waiter said. "I would not go to the police for . . . for various reasons, but everyone knows that the lady—Miss Rowan—has been asking many questions and writing in the papers. It is known you protect the names of those who speak to you, miss, so that is why—tonight—I decided to come and see you." He looked up at Simon. "Of course I did not know you would be here."

The Saint acknowledged the statement with a noncommittal nod.

"I'm very grateful that you've come," Tammy said. "Go ahead."

Mahmud's youthful face reflected all the impotent shame and rage of a man crushed by arrogant forces hopelessly stronger than himself.

"It was not an accident that broke my arm," he said in a voice that shook with emotion. "They broke it. They broke it on purpose. They threw me on the floor, and with his foot . . ." Mahmud stopped, his head hanging, and took new control of himself. When he started talking again it was directly to Tammy. "I know people have spoken to you about the man that calls himself Kalki, the big one that wrestles. He did this to me."

Simon and Tammy exchanged glances of controlled triumph.

"Why did they pick on you this time?" the Saint asked quietly.

"I was a friend of Ali's. Not a close friend. He had no close friends. But they did not know how close we might be. They killed Ali because he was going to tell all about them to the police. They . . . did this to me as a warning, and because I had argued when they last wanted me to pay them."

"Pay them for what?" Tammy asked.

Mahmud adjusted his position and for a moment his face twisted with pain.

"Many people pay them," he said. "For nothing." He directed his next few words to Tammy again. "You have written about this. You know. They bring Pakistani people into England and promise them good papers and jobs, and then when such people are here they are told they will be reported to the police and sent to jail if they do not pay."

"That's not a very accurate interpretation of the illegal entry laws," Simon said.

"Many people do not know the law. They do not know English. They do not care about what the law says—they are just frightened. Very scared." He shook his head. "And it does not matter about the law anyway. The ones who want the money will take it no matter what you know about the law. I was not afraid of the immigration authorities, but these men took a part of my money each week. After what had happened to Ali—and me—nobody will have courage not to pay them."

"Besides the two characters from that delivery van, who else is in on the collecting side of this operation?" the Saint asked.

Mahmud's English, or his nerve, failed him briefly at that point.

"I am not sure what you mean," he said with a puzzled expression.

"Who runs the gang?" Simon said. "Who's the boss?"

The Pakistani's mouth twitched with spasmic tension before he finally answered.

"I do not know for sure who is the highest man," he said hesitantly. "But I know one higher than Kalki."

Mahmud bogged down again, so Simon urged him on.

"And who is that?"

"Someone you know: Abdul Haroon, the man who owns the Golden Crescent."

4

The Saint had known enough evildoers of improbable shapes, sizes, temperaments, and professions to be surprised at almost nothing, but Tam Rowan's journalistic endeavours had apparently not given her quite as much sophistication.

"You mean that nervous little fat man?" she gasped.

"Yes, miss," replied Mahmud.

Having revealed Abdul Haroon's darker nature, the slim waiter now looked like a man who had uttered some unforgivable blasphemy and was expecting violent and noisy electrical disturbances of the atmosphere directly above his head.

"He's the one who gives the orders to the people who collect the money?" Tammy asked.

"Yes. Higher than him is an Englishman, I think, but I do not know his name or anything about him."

Simon was completely intrigued by the whole situation now, and began to think better of the whim that had led him to become involved. He folded his arms and faced the Pakistani.

"Tell us everything else you know about the way they work," he told Mahmud. "How do you know Mr Haroon is one of the gang leaders? Is there any kind of concrete evidence?"

Mahmud's eyes flashed again, and his voice was shrill with emotion.

"They have broken my arm!" he said. "They have killed Ali. Do you need more evidence than that?"

"I think Mr Templar means the kind of evidence we could show to the police or use in court," Tammy intervened soothingly.

Mahmud began struggling with his unbroken arm to heave himself to his feet.

"I should not have come here," he winced. "I do not want to see police and go in courts! I . . ."

Simon stepped forward and placed a strong hand on the waiter's shoulder, easing him back in the chair.

"You don't have to see the police," he said. "We could all be fossils before Scotland Yard and the lawyers and the judges and unrestricted-immigration left wing and every bovine bureaucrat in the country got through gnawing on a case like this. Miss Rowan and I are great believers in independent action. Tell us everything you know and we'll do the rest."

"I have told you almost everything," Mahmud responded. "Mr Haroon and Kalki and the others, they scare Pakistani people to make them pay money, and if they do not pay they are beaten. Kalki and the little American called Shortwave collect the money."

Simon was looking at him intently.

"Do you know anybody else who could give us information?" he asked.

Mahmud shook his head despondently.

"Nobody will tell anything." He paused, then looked up. "I have one more information. It might be very important. Just before you came into the restaurant this evening, Mr Templar, I heard something that Kalki and Mr Haroon said. Mr Haroon is going—tonight—to meet with the Englishman who is also high in the gang."

Tammy leaned forward, brushing her blonde hair away from her face.

"Where?"

"At the Grey Goose—a pub near Datchet." Mahmud tapped his forehead. "I made certain that I remembered it."

He began to give directions for driving to the pub which he had heard Kalki relay to Abdul Haroon, but the Saint cut him short.

"It just happens that I know it. I collect pubs for a hobby, and I probably know every one in the Thames Valley. The Grey Goose is a real old-fashioned country 'local,' right off the beaten track—I don't suppose they sell two pints a week to anyone from beyond walking distance. If they were looking for a place where they wouldn't stand one chance in a million of being seen by anyone who knew them, they couldn't have picked a better one."

"If Haroon needs directions it obviously isn't a regular meeting place," Tammy objected.

"Maybe they never meet in the same place twice."

"I think that they do not often meet," Mahmud put in. "Two—maybe three times I have heard Mr Haroon speak on the telephone to a man who must be the Englishman . . . but I do not know any more."

"What did they talk about?" Simon asked.

The waiter made a vague gesture.

"When will people be coming in on the boat . . . how much money Haroon is to get . . . such things as that."

"This is the boat that smuggles the immigrants into England?" Tammy asked.

Mahmud was showing signs of almost painful weariness in addition to his nervous fear.

"I do not know," he sighed. "I do not know more. I have told everything—and now they will kill me."

He began to make feeble efforts to get up again, and Simon thought it best to let him leave if he wanted to. He gave the Pakistani a helping hand and steadied him when he was standing.

"They won't kill you because of anything we let them know," Simon assured him. "I suppose you made sure nobody followed you."

"Yes. I was very sure."

"Where can we take you?" Tammy asked. She glanced at the Saint. "My car just has room for two."

"And I came by taxi," Simon said.

Mahmud interrupted.

"I would not want to have the danger that somebody would see me with you," he insisted. "It is better that I go in a taxi. If you would please ring for one . . ."

"Of course," Tammy said, and picked up the phone.

"I do not think I can walk until I come to a busy road where I could find one," the waiter said apologetically as she dialled.

"Don't worry about it," the Saint told him. "You were a brave man to come here, especially after what happened to you tonight."

"I was angry," Mahmud said. "I thought I would rather be dead than lie still while they walked on me and broke my bones." He leaned tiredly against the wall next to the door. "And what will you do?" he asked. "You will help?"

Simon nodded.

"I think I'll do a little country pub-crawling."

"We, not I," Tammy put in. She looked sympathetically at Mahmud. "The taxi's on its way. Would you like a drink or something?"

"No, thank you. I will go down and wait. Please do not come with me."

Tammy opened the door.

"How can we get in touch with you?"

"I have no telephone," the Pakistani said. "It is best if you do not try to see me at all. I have come here and told you all I know, but I do not want more trouble."

Tammy asked him to telephone her if he found out anything new.

"I will," he promised, "but for some weeks I will be not working. A waiter who cannot write orders or carry trays is no good waiter."

He managed a faint smile and then said good night and walked very slowly away towards the stairs.

"Should we just let him go like that?" Tammy said sotto voce when she had closed the door again. "I mean, he's so weak."

"He's right about not wanting to risk being seen with us," Simon said. "Your room is on the front. Turn out the light and we can watch from the window and at least be sure he gets into his taxi with no trouble. I assume he won't have much walking to do when it drops him wherever his room is."

"Oh, Lord, I should have asked him where he lives," Tammy said.

"I don't think he'd have told us," the Saint replied matter-of-factly. "Now let's get that light out and have a look."

Tammy flicked off the living-room lights leaving the flat in darkness. The only illumination now came from the street lamps outside. Simon went to the window and partially drew aside the curtain.

"Is he down there yet?" Tammy asked.

"He's just coming out," the Saint reported.

The girl came and stood beside him so that she could share his view of the sidewalk. When she realised that her shoulder was pressing against his she edged quickly away.

"He's pretty brave to do this, you know," she commented a little nervously.

"Yes. Almost too brave."

Tammy nodded in agreement. Mahmud was a somehow pathetically small shadow among other shadows at the edge of the garden that bordered the street. The lights and then the black gleaming shape of a taxi came into sight and slowed in front of the house.

"Lord," Tammy said tensely, as if she half expected the quietness of her neighbourhood to erupt into an ear-shattering exhibition of submachine-gun fire in the grandest Chicago tradition.

But Mahmud only climbed with painful slowness into the taxi and then was driven unspectacularly away. Tammy breathed again and Simon spoke.

"I'll be going, then. Thanks very much for the talk—and the exercise."

"We'll be going, and that's the last time I intend to correct you," Tammy said. "Let me change into a skirt and grab my purse. Have you got any money? I never do. You didn't bring your car?"

"Yes, I do have some money, and no, I didn't bring my car. Do you have one?"

"Yes. That's one reason why I don't have any money. With my wheels and your cash we should go a long way, though. Ready?"

"Eminently."

"Onward, the Light Brigade," Tammy said. "Into the jaws of death, into the mouth of hell, or whatever the poet said."

"Don't forget, he was also a prophet," Simon remarked.

They had just stepped into the hall, and Tammy locked the door behind her.

"What is that ominous statement supposed to mean?" she asked.

"I know we made a deal," Simon answered, "but as the older and possibly more clearheaded member of this partnership I think I ought to remind you that instead of being the toast of Fleet Street when this expedition is over, you may end up as dead as Ali, and just as uncomfortably."

"Rot!" Tammy said defiantly. "We'll see who's the most clear-headed. Come on."

"I think I'd better remind you of something else," Simon told her as she started off down the hall.

"What?"

"You forgot to put on your shoes."

CHAPTER THREE:

HOW SHORTWAVE WAS RECEPTIVE AND MAHMUD LOST HIS HIS COOL

1

When Tam Rowan had gone back into her flat and returned to the Saint properly shod, the two of them walked quietly downstairs to the entrance hall.

"Much more practical," Simon said with a glance at her low-heeled brown shoes. "And I congratulate you on your presence of mind: they're both the same colour."

She compressed her lips and did not say anything. He stopped her with a touch on her arm as she headed for the door.

"Is there a back way out of this place?" he asked. "Just in case some of your fans are watching in front."

"Of course," she said haughtily. "This way."

She led him down the hall into its dark nether regions and disengaged the bolt which held the rear door shut. They stepped out into a tiny fenced yard where the apartment building's wastepaper and orange peels overflowed several containers.

"Through here," she pointed.

They went through an opening in the wooden fence and were standing in a narrow cul-de-sac just wide enough to allow a row of cars to park along one side and still leave access for driving in and out.

"We can walk around and catch a taxi," Simon said. "My car's at my flat."

"Mine's right here," Tammy said. "Let's take it. There's no point in wasting time."

"Okay."

She took him to a long, low, scarlet sports car with gleaming wire-spoke wheels.

"Very nice," the Saint said.

"Thank you. It'll be mine in another eight hundred and forty-five payments—assuming I can come up with enough dirt on this immigration racket to keep my boss doling out the wherewithal."

Simon opened her door for her and went around to jackknife himself into the low bucket seat on the other side.

"I wonder if you couldn't have bought something a little more roomy for eight hundred and forty-six payments," he commented.

"The littler they are the more fun they are to scoot around in," she said. "You obviously weren't designed for overpopulated areas."

"I'm strictly designed for wide open spaces," he agreed. "Shall we try the ignition and see what happens?"

She reached for the key, then hesitated, looking at him in the dim greenish light of the instrument panel.

"What do you mean, see what happens?"

"See if it blows up in our faces," he elucidated.

"Are you insulting my car or are you implying there might be a bomb planted in the engine?" she asked uncertainly.

"The latter, but I don't think your sparring partners are that technologically advanced. You're much more likely to get a knife between your charmingly upholstered ribs, or a piano-wire collar around your neck."

She swallowed audibly.

"I'm going to start it," she threatened, as if hoping that he would stop her.

"Go ahead. Take a chance."

She turned the key with stabbing determination. The engine coughed and burbled to a steady rumble. There was, as Simon had expected, no explosion. Tammy took a deep breath and presented him with a triumphant look.

"So there," she said. "Satisfied?"

"Alive," he said. "And that's good enough for me. Let's go."

She backed the car out of the cul-de-sac and he directed her to circle the block to avoid passing in front of the building.

"If the subjects of your biographical essays happen to be watching your front door, this may help us to give them the slip," Simon explained. "On the other hand, unless they're totally incompetent, they could be watching the back too, but there's no harm in trying."

"Do you really think somebody might follow us?"

Simon meditated on her snub-nosed, tense-lipped profile for a few seconds.

"You always sound so surprised at these things," he remarked. "Don't you have any idea at all of what you've gotten yourself into?"

"Of course I do!" she retorted. "Don't worry about me. I'll be fine." She slowed down and then continued irritably. "What's the best way to Datchet?"

"The shortest way you know from here to the M4, for a start."

He kept a sharp lookout while she steered them southwards through a minimum of traffic to join the major westward motorway. The suburban commuters and shoppers were safely home, and it would be some time before the theatre goers started back.

"At this hour, we should make it comfortably in thirty minutes," he said.

"There's one thing neither one of us has mentioned," Tammy said.

She seemed less tense now that they were putting a good distance between themselves and her flat. The Saint, finally satisfied that nobody was following the red sports car, settled more comfortably in his own incapacious seat.

"What's that?" he asked.

"The police," she said in fateful tones.

"There are lots of other things we haven't mentioned either," Simon said, stretching out his long arm across the back-rest behind her shoulders. "Popcorn, Mount Fujiyama, Ivan the Terrible . . ."

"Oh, you're impossible!"

He was smiling at her.

"It's true, I am," he said modestly. "And I apologise for not mentioning the police. What would you like me to mention about them? Their social usefulness, their handsome uniforms, their unfailing graciousness, their martyrdom at the hands of bearded baboons breaking up park benches for holy causes?"

"Why can't you be serious? People are getting their arms broken and all you can do is make jokes."

"That's not all I'm doing. I'm putting my life in the hands of a woman driver. Greater love hath no man. What about the police?"

"Shouldn't we tell them what's going on?"

"It's their job to know what's going on," Simon said. "They have nothing else to do for twenty-four hours a day but poke around finding out what's going on. If we know more than they do, it hardly makes me feel they're deserving of our help. Besides, what could we tell them? We've got nothing they could take action on."

"But we might get in trouble."

The Saint nodded complacently.

"We undoubtedly will."

"With the police, I mean."

"That too," he concurred. "Especially considering how much they already love me for my past services."

He watched her face in the irregular play of lights that swept continuously through the car. She looked as if she was beginning to have doubts about the bargain she had made.

"You've been in trouble with them before, haven't you?" she asked.

"Oh, yes."

"You've stolen things, haven't you . . . and killed people."

"I have been known to supplement the efforts of the State to balance the distribution of wealth and do justice as it should be done."

"And I had to get myself mixed up with you!"

"I shall try to prove that I'm not a total liability. Love, of course, may take a little longer to burgeon."

That silenced her until they were past the exit to Heathrow Airport, and may have added some helpful weight to the pressure of her foot on the accelerator. The Saint was not alarmed, for by that time he had been able to rate her as a fast and proficient driver, and for a while he was satisfied to let her concentrate on that.

After he estimated that her blood-pressure should be close to normal again, he said, "Just to pass the time, I'd like to hear more about this Kalki the Kook who does the bone-breaking bit."

"Kalki? What about him?"

"That's my question. What else do you know?"

Tammy made a perceptible effort to meet him on the same impersonal plane.

"He came to England about ten years ago, before there were many restrictions on commonwealth immigration. He has no police record, but they say he used to pad his income as a wrestler and lorry driver by meeting new arrivals from Pakistan at the airport, offering to help them, and then charging them a small fortune for a ride to their destination, where he dumped them and disappeared."

"Charming fellow," said Simon. "And now he's fishing in more troubled waters. Anything else?"

"That's about it on Kalki." Tammy pulled out to pass a convoy of three lumbering trucks. "Do you really know where we're going?" she asked.

"Yes. We take the next exit—it's marked 'A331 Slough-Colnbrook.' Meanwhile, what's the dossier on Kalki's sidekick? American, ex-jockey, what else?"

"Crazy as a loon, for a start," Tammy replied. "He fell off a horse years ago and cracked his skull. The doctors took a piece of bone out of his cranium and roofed him over with a stainless steel plate. Ever since then he claims he can pick up wireless broadcasts, and that's why they call him Shortwave." She laughed. "You don't believe me, do you?"

"Oh, I do. Fascinating. A human radio."

"So he says, and it may even be true. I had a close-up look at him at a pub one afternoon when I first started prowling around Soho, and he was giving everybody the latest odds from Ascot."

"Right off the top of his head, so to speak," mused Simon. "A mobile betting shop. If we can bring him back alive maybe we can sell him to Ladbrokes. What are his other distinctions besides access to the radio waves?"

"He likes hurting people," Tammy said flatly. "And he'll do anything for money. But as far as I know, he's just a tool."

"I wonder if he needs to be plugged in before he operates," Simon ruminated.

"Considering the kind of operations he's supposed to perform on people, I'd just as soon not find out," Tammy said. "In fact, I'm beginning to wonder if I won't ask the editor to transfer me to the cookery page."

The Saint chuckled.

"Don't chicken out now," he told her. "We've got some three-star thrills to look forward to. Just think of it: super-thug and his marvellous electronic midget. That combination beats steak-and-kidney pie any day. Here's our turn-off, coming up now."

"I saw it," Tammy said in a grim voice.

"You're welcome to hitch a ride back to town if you feel a little nervous," Simon said maliciously. "Just let me borrow your baby hot-rod, and I'll give you an exclusive interview when the rough stuff's over."

The lights of an approaching car flared across the girl's face as she came down to the roundabout at the bottom of the exit ramp. Her face was tense with the determination of a novice high-wire walker about to give her first performance without benefit of net.

"Never mind," she said, between what Simon imagined were clenched teeth. "Just never mind the comical comments! I'll be right with you through the 'Hallelujah Chorus.'" She slowed the car. "What next?"

"Bear that way, where the little sign says "Datchet." Then look out for another side marker that says "Wraysbury" . . . From here on, if you won't let me take over, you'll have to let me side-seat drive . . ."

He continued his coolly confident pilotage, even when an unlikely turning into which he had ordered her became a narrow track which dipped, twisted, and writhed through a thick coppice as if its original course had been charted by a drink-crazed Hottentot on the trail of a devious wart hog.

It bored its tortuous way under a tunnel-like covering of trees for a quarter of a mile before the tenuous strip of mud and gravel shook itself, straightened, and took off like an arrow between two open fields.

"I hope you really do know this road," Tammy said sceptically, and pressed the accelerator almost to the floor.

Simon heard one rifle shot over the steepening roar of the engine, and then the explosion of the left front tyre. Tammy screamed as her car tried to leap from under them like a shying horse.

2

At the instant of its skid the red sports car became a hurtling missile instead of a vehicle. All the Saint could do was to grab the steering wheel and keep Tammy from giving it a hysterical overcorrection that would have launched the car into a series of flips and turned its occupants into little more than unsightly stains on the upholstery.

The infuriating sense of powerlessness that overwhelmed him was at least short-lived. The buck and swerve of the car, the squeal of the tyres, the crazy Cossack dance of a hedge in the sweeping headlights, were all over in a jagged lightning-flash of time that ended in a strangely anticlimactic muffled thud, and total darkness.

The darkness, too, lasted a very short time. Even while the Saint was half stunned, every cell in his brain was struggling for life, clawing back to full consciousness. The distant sound of the rifle shot that had made the car veer off the road still echoed in his skull like a shouted word of warning bouncing down and down through a nerve-net of subterranean chambers. A less experienced, less finely tuned mind would not even have separated out and identified the gunshot for what it was; it would have been merely a meaningless part of the panic-fused sensation of what would later have been recognised as an automobile accident.

But for Simon the explosive crack still resounding in his head was a call to arms as clear as the blast of a trumpet. Unfortunately even his perfectly conditioned body was not immune to the effects of being thrown, encapsuled in steel, into a ditch at seventy miles an hour. It took him a few seconds to come fully back to awareness, and by that time the most prominent thing he became aware of was the long slender black snout of a rifle poking down through the car's open window at the side of his head.

The lights had gone out, but the moon was bright, and when Simon's eyes travelled up the barrel of the rifle to focus on the man who held it he had no trouble at all in recognising the face of none other than Mahmud the waiter, whose right arm was conspicuously free of splints, white bandages, or a sling.

"Are they d-d-d-dead?" inquired a rather thin male voice from offstage.

"No," Mahmud answered with frank dissatisfaction.

"And the lame shall take up their guns and walk," Simon said biblically.

The voice from the darkness of the car startled Mahmud, who jerked back, aiming the rifle more tensely.

"Go ahead—shoot them," came the thin voice.

"No. Pull the girl out. And you come out, Mr Templar, with your hands in front of you."

The car had run into the shallow ditch at an angle, and it had come to rest with its right side higher than its left side. Simon was on the lower side. When he turned to look at Tammy she was already being half-dragged, half-helped out of the driver's seat. Too dazed to comprehend what was happening, she put up no resistance. Simon might have tried some resistance of his own except for the fact that she was in the hands of the opposition before he had been able to fully collect his own resources.

"Out!" Mahmud repeated.

His voice was more frightened than menacing which Simon took to be a dangerous state of affairs. He would much rather have faced a calm professional killer than a scared amateur who might pull the trigger without even knowing it.

The Saint, accordingly, opened his door the short distance that the car's inclined position allowed and squeezed himself out onto the soft damp cushion of leaves that filled the ditch. Mahmud moved back above the rim of the ditch, keeping the rifle pointed straight at Simon's chest. Around the front of the car came Tammy, pushed by a man almost a head shorter than she was—the same man Simon had seen in the alley behind the Golden Crescent with the giant wrestler.

"What's happening?" she asked groggily.

"Our friend Mahmud here has experienced a miraculous recovery and couldn't wait for us to share his joy with him—so he shot out one of your front tyres and precipitated us into this pleasant glen." He smiled at the tense Pakistani. "Good shooting, Mahmud, and how about introducing me to your faith healer?"

"Well, go on and do something!" squeaked the little man who was holding Tammy in accents that had more of Chicago than London in them. "They didn't get killed, so you gotta kill 'em!"

"If I shoot, the police will know why it was done," Mahmud said. "It must look like an accident, Kalki said."

"Beat 'em on the head, then!" his partner pleaded. "Do something! Bash 'em with your gun butt! Just hurry up. I see lights! I see lights coming!"

"Through the hedge, quick!" Mahmud said. "Everybody, or I do shoot. This way."

Tammy gave a faint yelp as her captor doubled one of her arms behind her back and shoved her stumbling up the side of the ditch. Simon followed at a more leisurely pace, looking over his shoulder to confirm for himself that the headlights of a car were flickering through the trees from a nearby bend in the road. If it had not been for Tammy he would have pitted his own speed and agility against Mahmud's nervous marksmanship, but as it was, all he could do was follow her through a gap in the straggly quickset and reflect on the instinctive wisdom which had led sailors through the centuries to regard a woman on shipboard as an infallible omen of disaster.

"Get your hands off me, you ape!" the female herself was protesting dizzily. "Where do you think we're going?"

Nobody, including the Saint, bothered to answer her. They had hurried some distance into the field when Mahmud had ordered them all down on their knees. On the road, the lights of the approaching car zipped past without slowing. Mahmud started to stand up and then he squatted again as the sound of suddenly applied brakes squealed through the trees.

"They've seen it," said Tammy's diminutive escort. "Let's beat it out of here!"

Mahmud did not argue.

"Hurry!" he said. "Run! That way."

The Pakistani brought up the rear of the unevenly hasty procession, urging them on until Tammy almost collapsed for lack of breath.

"Over there," Mahmud said. "Do not stop."

Nowhere in that area is it possible to walk very far without coming to a road of some sort, and they soon reached the local limit of trackless wilderness. They came to a gate which let them out on to an unpaved lane. In a bay by the gate was a parked car. In the field opposite loomed the black shape of a barn. A gust of wind rattled branches overhead as the group stopped, and Mahmud peered anxiously through the darkness behind them. There were no sounds except the wind and Tammy's almost sobbing gasps for breath.

"We're okay now," said the diminutive American. "Let's finish with these characters and get out of here."

Simon studied the man in the dim light of the moon. His face was skeletally thin, crowned with hair about an inch long which stood rigidly straight up on end.

"You must be Shortwave," the Saint said cordially.

"You heard of me?" asked the little man with pleased surprise.

Simon nodded.

"What's the latest from Radio Three?"

Shortwave grinned.

"You wanna know what I heard while we was running across here?"

He began to whistle.

"Quiet!" Mahmud snapped at him. "Everyone get into the car."

"The finale of Beethoven's Ninth," Simon reflected on Shortwave's performance.

"Yeah?" said Shortwave happily. "I been picking up a lot of stuff from the Heathrow control tower lately too."

With his rifle, Mahmud was urging them into the parked Ford a few yards away. Shortwave produced a pistol from his baggy jacket.

"What's the idea?" he objected. "Shoot 'em here, an' we don't make a mess of the car."

"Now that it cannot look like an accident," Mahmud said impatiently, "it should be done where their bodies will not be found."

"So don't talk stupid," Simon amplified, for Shortwave's benefit.

A sharp stinging blow on the back of his neck knocked him forward. He blinked back the moisture that automatically flooded his eyes and turned to see Shortwave holding his pistol club-like and threatening on a level with his shoulder.

"We're gonna kill you," Shortwave said. "With pleasure."

"That's the method I'd prefer," Simon said evenly. "I'm going to kill you with anything I can get my hands on."

"Big deal!" said Shortwave scornfully. "You and what army?"

Mahmud prodded Simon into the front passenger seat, Tammy into the back, and directed Shortwave in beside her. It was a very different performance from anything he had ever put on at the Golden Crescent. He was still a nervous amateur, but he was finding reserves of competence which indicated a surprising affinity for his new vocation. He put the rifle in on the floor at Shortwave's feet, went around and got in behind the wheel, swung and reversed the car around, and took off at a bouncing speed down the uneven road.

"Stop talking so much," he said. "And believe me, Mr Templar, if you try to interfere with what we do your woman will suffer."

"I am not his woman," Tammy protested weakly.

"You'll be nothing if he starts acting up," said Shortwave. His next words were aimed at Mahmud. "Where are you going?"

"To the boathouse—it is the only thing," Mahmud answered. "But they should not be let to know where it is. Perhaps you will tie something across their eyes?"

Shortwave settled back comfortably in his corner of the back seat, cradling his pistol in both hands.

"Who cares if they know how to get to the boathouse?" he asked softly. "Once they get in there, they ain't never coming out."

3

Tammy Rowan, who had seemed partly dazed since her car had spun off the road, began to wake up completely to what was happening around her as Mahmud drove on a twisting route through the night.

"This is crazy!" she protested. "First somebody's got a smashed arm and then he doesn't. My car has a blowout and two goons with guns just happen to be waiting by the side of the road . . ."

Simon had contrived to turn sideways with his back to the door so that he could see Mahmud, Shortwave, and—without unduly twisting his neck—Tammy, who was directly behind him.

"I'm sure your feminine intuition and/or your nose for news can set you on the path to figuring it all out," he said unindulgently.

She paused sullenly to think things over.

"Right," she sighed. "And I suppose they were responsible for wrecking my car somehow too."

"Mahmud did it with his little popgun," Simon said. "Didn't you, Mahmud? I heard the shot just as the tyre went. Did you develop your aim in the Khyber Pass or a shooting gallery in Blackpool, comrade?"

Mahmud stared silently ahead.

"Talkative lad," the Saint commented. He regarded Mahmud with scientific interest as he continued. "I have a feeling that the bigger fish in his scummy little pond have got something on him, otherwise he'd be peacefully pushing brinjal pickle for Mr Haroon. He doesn't look like a criminal type to me. No nerve."

"Be quiet," Mahmud said ineffectually.

Shortwave, relaxed and confident with his gun clasped between his hands, giggled from the back seat.

"So this guy really is the Saint?" he chortled. "What a laugh. It was all too easy."

"As easy as falling off a log," Simon agreed. "But don't laugh too much till after you've landed."

Shortwave giggled appreciatively again and fondled his pistol. Tammy could not share the surface geniality.

"Mahmud!" she interrupted. "Or whatever your name is. Listen—if this lot is forcing you into something, we can help you. Take us back to town and we'll see that you're protected." She glanced at Shortwave. "Both of you. You don't run this gang. If you'll help us catch them, we'll back you up when the thing goes to court."

Mahmud shook his head and told her again to stop talking. Shortwave merely tittered.

"There's just one thing I'm curious about," Simon said to Mahmud. "Why did you decide to stage that faked broken arm while I was at the Golden Crescent? Don't tell me; let me guess. Because you panicked when I started asking questions and thought I was on to you—so you decided nothing could be more certain to throw me off the trail than making it look as if you were getting broken to bits for going against the gang. With you in the clear, the bigger boys could use you to steer Miss Rowan—or me—just where they wanted us. And a neat little ambush you made of it, for a rush job. There's only one road we could take to the Grey Goose, and you had enough of a start to be there waiting for us."

"He's real bright, ain't he?" Shortwave remarked. "So bright he's about to get a hole blown in his head."

Simon regarded him indulgently.

"What fun!" he drawled. "And when it's been repaired like yours, we'll be able to communicate, like satellites."

As they cut across the town centre of Staines, Mahmud reiterated a warning.

"Please don't try anything foolish, Mr Templar, or Miss Rowan will receive the consequences from Shortwave."

Simon did not need the reminder. A lively awareness of the risk to Tammy was what had forced him to let this pair of bush-league bandits get away with some manoeuvres which, if he had been on his own, might have brought an abrupt end to their careers.

They left Staines by the Laleham road, and continued on to Shepperton, but a mile or two beyond that Mahmud took a sharp fork into a complex of winding lanes that soon had the Saint straining his directional memory. It was an area which he might not have recognised even in daylight, for it had the unfinished air of recent development: still unpaved roads cut between glimpses of old houses abandoned before the spread of raw excavations. The mention of a "boathouse" meant the river, and this seemed to be one of those sections where the gravel pits which had not long destroyed it were being painfully salvaged as new residential waterfront and small-boat marinas.

The boathouse which they came to eventually, after bumping over a rutted track across a grassy field, had obviously once been an appendage of some gracious estate of which the main building was not to be seen, if it still stood. The boathouse, naturally, stood on the very edge of the river, and was big enough to contain an apartment on the upper floor, where lights showed in the windows.

"We're here," Mahmud said superfluously. "No one must move until I tell you."

He steered the car around to the far side of the building, the headlights sweeping over dark bricks which could easily have been a hundred years old, and brought them on to the old driveway which had once served it, which now lost itself in weeds and bushes a few yards inland.

Another vehicle was already there: the van that Simon had seen in the alley behind the Golden Crescent that afternoon.

"What do you think—is this the headquarters of the whole Koo-Koo Klan?" Simon said to Tammy. "Or just a substation?"

Mahmud cut off the engine of the car and then the headlights. The light that came from the windows above was weak and yellow.

"Now," he said. "Do what I tell you. Sit here and wait. I will go inside for a minute."

"Let's take 'em on in," Shortwave said. "What the hell do we need to wait for?"

"Scared of the dark?" the Saint sympathised. "We'll be here to keep you company."

"I must ask," Mahmud told his accomplice. He jerked his head towards the house. "He does not know we bring them here."

Shortwave looked slightly apprehensive.

"Yeah. It's your fault. I told you we oughta conk 'em and leave 'em there like it was an accident."

"We couldn't," Mahmud said almost desperately. "There were cars coming. This was all we could do!"

"Tell it to him, not me," Shortwave replied, indicating the house once again. "It's your show. I'm just riding shotgun."

"Loyalty to the end," commented Simon. "Doesn't it grab you, Tammy?"

Mahmud opened his door and got out. Shortwave was no longer slouching relaxed in his corner of the back seat as he had been during the ride. He sat up straight and alert, holding the pistol on Tammy with his right hand while he steadied his right forearm with the other.

"There's just about one spider web between this dame and the Great Beyond," he said to Simon, "so sit tight and don't try nothing."

"Why should I try anything?" the Saint asked languidly. "What more could I ask? Free transportation, fresh country air, brilliant conversation . . ."

Shortwave grunted, keeping on his guard, his eyes narrowed. Then he began to hum a nervous mournful gipsy tune.

"And thou beside me singing in the wilderness," Simon added. "Our very own portable radio."

Tammy Rowan, who was so busy trying to look brave that she could hardly move, glanced at Shortwave, who appeared to have sunk into a state of trance. His thin reedy humming went on. His eyelids drooped, but Simon could see that the dilated black pupils peered out of his skeletal face with undiminished watchfulness.

Tammy spoke very softly and hesitantly, as if she thought Shortwave were asleep and might not hear if she kept her voice down.

"What are we going to do?"

Shortwave, as motionless as a coiled snake, went on with his humming.

"We'll do just as we're told," the Saint replied. "Don't be fooled by Shortwave's gentle manner and wholesome demeanour: I have a feeling he can be pretty nasty if he gets riled."

Shortwave chuckled suddenly.

"You're damn right."

"I didn't mean to interrupt the programme," Simon told him.

"I was gettin' Radio Luxembourg," Shortwave informed him in return. "It comes in real clear about this time."

There had not been any sounds from inside the boathouse, but now a door apparently opened, letting out into the night a babble of at least two excited and irritated non-English voices. Feet crunched along the drive towards the car, and Mahmud opened the door beside Shortwave.

"Bring them into the house," he ordered. "Hurry!"

"Okay," Shortwave said. "You guys cool it now and do like I say. I'm gonna back out of here, and you follow me out this door, girlie. Saint, you hold it right where you are till I give you the word to move—unless you want her to get hurt."

He kept his pistol in thoroughly professional readiness while he slipped out of the car and Mahmud retrieved his rifle from the vacated floor. The Saint had decided as soon as he was captured that unless a really good chance presented itself he would not try to escape or otherwise turn the tables until he had been taken to the group's headquarters. Mahmud, in deciding to drive him straight to the boathouse, might have been saving him a good bit of work—while a minor slip could have cost Tammy Rowan's life.

Now one objective seemed to have been reached, and the next few moments could very well give him the best chance to make his move. Mahmud, in his jittery state, had not even thought to search the Saint for weapons, but even if he had made the conventional search, he would quite likely have failed to find Anna, the slim beautifully balanced throwing knife in the sheath strapped to his left forearm. It was a card up the Saint's sleeve that more professional friskers had overlooked before, and the fingertips of Simon's right hand casually located the hilt of it while he considered how long he could most effectively wait before bringing it into play.

But then, as Mahmud took a step back and waited for the girl to follow as reluctantly as it would have been natural to expect, the Saint's carefully cultivated restraint was nullified by another factor over which he had no control. Tammy Rowan, in some excess of reckless bravery, or some frantic irrational panic brought on by the prospect of rapidly approaching doom, hurled herself from her seat and dived for the rifle. The effort might have made more sense if the trigger end had not been in Mahmud's hands, leaving Tammy in unpromising possession of the barrel.

Even in the first second of the grim tug-of-war Simon knew what the outcome would be, but he felt he had no choice but to go on the offensive himself. Mahmud was shouting, and Shortwave started around the car to try to cut off any escape attempt from the other side. Expecting at any moment to hear the crack of the rifle as it was fired point-blank in the scuffle, Simon shouted at Tammy to let go and give up. Then he vigorously opened his door just in time for it to catch Shortwave full in the face as he came scampering around the front of the car.

As Shortwave crashed to a standstill, Simon rolled out and grabbed him. Mahmud was screeching at Tammy in his native tongue, and a thudding of heavy footsteps from the boathouse hinted that reinforcements were on the way. Either Mahmud had orders to keep Tammy alive, or he did not want to put holes in his car, or his rifle had jammed: for some reason the shot Simon kept expecting still did not come. On his own battle-front he disarmed Shortwave by chopping his wrist with the edge of one hand and knocking the pistol to the ground. Shortwave yowled and kicked and flailed like a human buzzsaw, trying to counter the Saint's superior strength and skill with sheer wild motion. The Saint calculated carefully for a split second and then sent his fist shooting into the human blur at just the proper instant to crack him hard on the point of his jaw.

Shortwave sagged against the side of the car. And then the Saint had a peculiar dreamlike sensation, experienced, it is almost certain, by few people besides Elijah and a handful of other mortals thought worthy by the Higher Powers of being borne bodily away to heaven without suffering the usual preliminaries. He felt himself lifted straight into the air, where he dangled for a moment before the less inspiring portion of his journey began. Then whatever had elevated him put him down. Threw him down would be a more accurate way of saying what was done to him—and what followed was even more unpleasant. He had just been jarred to the earth flat on his back when he got his first glimpse of the human colossus to whom he owed his experience, and whose gallon-capacity left shoe which introduced itself by crunching into his side between his ribs and his pelvis. At the same instant he heard the rifle finally fire.

4

For a few seconds of blinding pain he was completely incapacitated, and when he began to suck in breath again his hands were already being tied behind him. In the process, Anna was discovered and snatched from her sheath.

His first full awareness was the sight of Mahmud hurling Tammy to the ground with a whip-jerk of her arm. He was not sure whether she had been shot or not. The waiter's rifle lay in the dust, and for a second Simon thought the Pakistani was stooping to retrieve it. But when Mahmud pivoted and turned to Tammy again it was a supple green branch torn from a nearby shrub that he held in his hand. Apparently unwounded, she tried to scramble to her feet to get away but he slashed the three-foot switch down across her shoulders. She screamed and fell back to the ground.

"Simon! Please! Do something!"

The Saint could only curse his helplessness. His wrists were now tightly bound, and he was hauled to his feet by the giant who had lifted him into the air and thrown him down again. He knew without looking who that was—and how completely useless it would be to put up any struggle at this point. Tammy screamed as Mahmud raised his slender stick again and swept it in a whistling arc across the girl's back. She screamed again and writhed, face down, her skirt twisted up around her legs, trying to protect her head with both arms. Mahmud's next lash was aimed at the bare legs.

"Stop!" commanded the huge wrestler who was holding the Saint. "Somebody might hear. Get her in the house, idiot!"

Mahmud looked furiously confused and frustrated as he hesitated, and then tossed his stick aside. Simon felt that Mahmud's violence was not so much due to sadism or even loss of temper as it was to the feeling that he had lost face in front of Shortwave and Kalki and had taken the only way he could think of to reassert his masculinity.

"Stupid woman!" he spat at Tammy as he dragged her sobbing to her feet.

Shortwave had been sitting on the ground with his back propped against one of the car's front wheels without evincing any interest in anything that was happening.

"Come on!" Kalki yelled at him in a voice which was strangely lacking in depth considering the vast dimensions of the man who produced it. He looked like a bull fiddle and sounded like a scratchy viola. "Get up and get in the ruddy house!"

Shortwave looked up at him with glazed eyes, comprehended, and pulled himself to his feet. He was still too fuzzy from the Saint's punch to do anything more ambitious than perform a wobbling march behind Mahmud and Tammy to a side door of the boathouse. Simon brought up the rear, pushed by his gargantuan captor.

The ground level of the building, into which medium-sized boats might have been hauled out from the river through full-width roller doors, was apparently being converted to additional living accommodation. A newly built brick unpainted wall in it closed off a large part of it, and another wall had been started where a stairway led to the floor above. Kalki kicked aside a cement-encrusted hoe as he shoved the Saint towards a bare trestle table with a number of cheap wooden chairs around it.

"Sit!" Kalki said to Simon, pushing him into one of the chairs in the middle of the room. "Tie his feet!" he ordered Shortwave.

For the first time Simon could take a good look at the wrestler at close range, and in these cramped quarters he seemed even more impressive than he had in the alley or on television. His costume was more impressive, too. He had changed his workman's outfit for a charcoal-grey Edwardian suit with orange waistcoat and burgundy silk tie. His shoes were brightly polished and he smelled of Yardley's. The suit was too small for him, and a good deal of thick wrist dangled below the jacket cuffs, but the effect he created was no less awe-inspiring because of a few sartorial defects. He looked a bit like a gorilla in formal dress.

"I can't say I'm pleased to meet you, but I am surprised," Simon remarked. "We were just watching you smash up somebody on television. How did you get dressed and down here so quickly?"

Kalki's reaction immediately made it plain that he had at least one weakness commensurate with his size. He puffed up visibly with pride, glanced at Tammy to make sure that she was paying attention, and looked back down at the Saint.

"It was me you saw on the television," he said self-importantly. "On tape. I made that show last week."

"How about that?" Simon commented to Tammy. "We're house guests of a celebrity. Look where ambition and hard work will get you."

"It's gonna get you a fancy funeral," Shortwave said viciously. He planted himself in front of the Saint with a piece of rope in his hand. "When I get through with you, you'll wish you'd never seen me except on television."

"Talking of television," Simon said with impeccable good humour, "how does that come through on your chromium plate? Do you receive the picture as well, or only the sound effects?"

Shortwave glared at him with red eyes and raised the rope, but Kalki stopped him magisterially, taking pride in his own massive self-control.

"Not now," he said magnanimously. "I do not like the lady to see you hit a man who cannot fight back. Wait until Fowler comes, and if he says so, you can do what you like—for as long as you like."

The fairly efficient trussing to which Simon had been subjected was not enough to suppress the raising of an eyebrow.

"Fowler?" he echoed. "Who he?—if I may use the idiom."

"You will find out," Mahmud said, pushing Tammy into another chair.

"Let me do some more guessing," Simon said. "He's the great White Wizard who's doing so much for you poor benighted victims of race prejudice—and making a nice profit for himself, of course. He also has a useful-sized pleasure boat registered with the Thames Conservancy, but also perfectly capable of running downriver and out to sea to make pick-ups. There can only be two or three locks between here and tidewater . . . And this is where the immigrant cargo can be landed and wait to be tidily dispersed. Not exactly Ritz accommodation, but I can see you're working on that . . . I didn't notice the boat, though. Could it be somewhere down the Thames Estuary right now, picking up more passengers?"

Mahmud impassively finished tying Tammy's hands together in front of her. Stubbornly pretending not to listen, he betrayed his tortured anxiety about what he was hearing.

"Not like that," Shortwave said irritably. "Behind her."

Kalki intervened, happy to display his authority again.

"Do as you are," he said to Mahmud. "The lady will be very well."

"Oh yes, the lady will be very well," Tammy sighed. She looked utterly defeated, too disheartened even to be frightened any more. "What are you going to do with us?"

"You wanna hear?" Shortwave asked as he got up from tying the Saint's feet. "It might take me a couple of hours to tell you."

Kalki gave a leviathan shrug.

"Do not worry about it," he pontificated to Tammy. "You were expected to be dead now, so no matter what happens this is all extra time. Enjoy it."

"Thanks so much," Tammy sighed. Then she suddenly stared at Simon. "They wouldn't really do it, would they?" she asked in a tone of horrified realisation. "I mean kill us? I didn't mean anything like that. I just wanted a story."

"You wanted to see us in prison," Kalki said without any overt hostility. "You wrote bad things. We warned you." He twitched his jaw to one side in a *c'est-la-vie* mannerism that produced a quivering of his black whiskers and a sound of lightly grating teeth. "So."

The abrupt, formally regretful "so" was self-explanatory enough for Tammy, who shivered as if she had suddenly been touched by a ghost, and dropped her gaze to the floor. For the first time she looked desperately, hopelessly terrified. Then, without any pause for a transition of mood, Kalki wheeled around and moved on Mahmud like a towering thunderstorm.

"And you!" he bellowed. "You bloody fool! I tell you to kill these people and you bring them here! I should have really broken your arm!"

Mahmud cowered before his massive accuser, and Shortwave, blinking rapidly, attempted to blend with the naked walls.

"I did as well as I could," Mahmud protested. He looked ready to burst into tears. "I told them where to come—the only road they could use, so there would be no mistake. Then we waited behind the hedge, and I hit the tyre with the first shot! How can you blame me if the car did not crash in a way to kill them?"

That part of Kalki's face visible above his home-grown Black Forest had turned dark purple.

"But why did you not kill them there?"

"I told him, I told him!" Shortwave blurted. "I said bash 'em in the head and make it look like they was killed in the wreck, but he wouldn't d-d-d-d-do it!"

"Lights were coming," Mahmud cried. "There was no chance!"

"Lights?" Kalki keened unreasonably. "Lights?"

He seemed about to reach down and break Mahmud in half, but when that happy prospect failed to materialise Simon entered the conversation.

"I must say you boys have all bungled this thing beautifully," he said, in a tone of great good cheer. "You should have stuck to beating up kids for pennies, because as it is you're getting in way out of your depth. You obviously aren't up to handling the situation, and the next thing you know you'll be permanently enjoying England's hospitality in a granite guesthouse. But let me insert a note of optimism: it's not too late. If you repent now you can still save your skins."

"Big deal!" was Shortwave's scornful response.

"Shut up!" Kalki said to Shortwave, and Shortwave shut up.

The giant turned to Simon.

"You can talk all you want to but it will be no use," he said to his prisoner. "I do not want to listen to you." He spoke to Mahmud and Shortwave. "We will put them in the back room—there."

He opened the door in the new partition wall. Since the Saint's ankles as well as his wrists were now tied he had to be carried by Mahmud and Shortwave. One took his arms and the other his legs, and together they staggered with their burden into an unfurnished, unlighted room that may have been intended to serve as a dormitory. Kalki, who might more logically have shared the load, escorted Tammy—whose legs were still free—along the same route. When he came with her into the room he turned on the light, saw Simon deposited on his back by the wall, and ordered Mahmud to bring the lady a chair.

"You will not have to wait long," he said ominously, "but you may as well be comfortable."

Simon inch-wormed himself into a sitting position. He had already tested the efficiency of the knots and windings Shortwave had put around his wrists and had found them unfortunately beyond reproach.

"When is Abdul Haroon joining the party?" he asked as Mahmud brought in a chair from the kitchen.

Kalki's jutting brow contracted above the deep hollows of his eye sockets.

"Haroon?" he asked, obviously puzzled.

"When I was at the woman's flat I told them Haroon was one of your chiefs," Mahmud explained. "It helped make them not suspicious about me."

The Saint had doubted that part of Mahmud's story as soon as he had heard it, but had wanted to check and be sure.

"Haroon!" Kalki said contemptuously. "That ball of pig fat! The only things he wants are more customers and cheaper meat. The day he has the courage to break a fly's wing I will jump over the Thames."

"It might do the world more good if you jumped in," Simon opined.

Kalki pointed a cudgel-sized finger at him—a theatrical gesture of warning accompanied by tilted head which the Saint had seen him use against his opponent in the televised wrestling match.

"And you might enjoy your short time of life more if you kept your mouth shut," the giant said.

He bent down and with a deliberate, almost stiffly performed movement, struck Simon a stinging blow across the face with the back of his hand. The Saint knew how to soften the effect with a subtly timed yielding of his head, but Kalki's hand was as big as an encyclopedia and the walnut-sized knuckles which adorned the back of it were a face-full to be reckoned with. As the Saint sat, steadily meeting the Pakistani's eyes and refusing to show the slightest sign of discomfort, he tasted the salty blood that oozed from the corner of his mouth where the blow had smashed the inner tissue against his teeth.

"Be sure there is nothing more in his pockets," Kalki told Mahmud. "Then leave them here until I have talked to Captain Fowler."

He stalked haughtily from the room, followed by Shortwave, while Mahmud carried out a perfunctory and ungentle search. Then Simon and Tammy were left alone.

"He's hurt you!" Tammy said, staring aghast at the Saint's face. "Why do you insist on making them angry? You scared me half to death."

The Saint looked around at the bare room, the stained plaster of three of its walls, the one window so thick with ancient grime and cobwebs that a curtain would have made it no more opaque. He looked at it as a stranded traveller accustomed to comfort might have looked at the last available room in some remote shanty town. Tammy's face, as she followed the direction of his eyes, reflected a more appalled sense of the awful novelty of the situation.

"I just thought I'd have a little fun with them," Simon said casually.

"A little fun?" his companion exclaimed. "They might have killed you."

"They intend to kill me anyway." He looked at her sharply. "And what about you, Miss Prudence? Jumping for that rifle in the car wasn't exactly the most discreet move I've ever seen. In fact it was downright stupid. How is it you aren't sporting a powder-lined perforation in your pinafore right now?"

"I thought maybe it wasn't loaded," she said, "and I kept away from the hole in the front while I was pulling on it . . ."

"The hole in the front?" the Saint repeated incredulously.

"The hole in the front of the gun," Tammy explained. "You know."

"Sometimes known as the barrel?" Simon said.

"Right. Where the shell comes out. And when he did shoot he didn't hit me, but it scared me so much I lost my grip."

"I'm thinking you lost your grip a little earlier, about the time you decided you were a crime reporter. But let's not worry about the past when we've got so little of the future ahead of us. Here we are, all bundled up, waiting for Fowler to view us before the *coup de grâce.* Thus endeth verse, page, chapter, and book, unless we can think of something to do."

"Who is this Captain Fowler?" Tammy asked.

"I don't know," said Simon. "Next question?"

"We could start yelling and screaming," Tammy suggested thoughtfully. "There might be a constable in the neighbourhood."

"Which vocal performance would last about five seconds, till our hosts got back and gagged us. Besides, I'm pretty sure there's nobody around these parts to hear us."

The girl lowered her voice almost to the point of inaudibility.

"I've still got my tear gas ring, and I reloaded it before we left my flat."

"That's good news," the Saint said. "Let the hostile legions tremble."

"Don't be sarcastic," she retorted. "It might work this time."

"It might be better than nothing," Simon admitted, without conviction, "and nothing is just about what we have to work with now . . ." He paused thoughtfully. "Unless it's that big ladykiller's swelled head."

"What do you mean?"

"I think Goliath may have an Achilles's heel, if you'll pardon the mixed mythology."

He did not go on. Tammy stared at him suddenly. A car was pulling into the drive and stopping outside the boathouse.

CHAPTER FOUR:

HOW CAPTAIN FOWLER WAS DISPLEASED AND ABDUL HAROON'S HOSPITALITY WAS IMPOSED ON

1

The Saint shot his blonde fellow-prisoner a silencing look and neither of them said anything. Above the sound of his own controlled breath, Simon listened for any clue that his ears might draw from the commonplace sounds outside the walls. Presumably the new arrival would be the co-conspirator referred to by Kalki as "Captain Fowler": if so, Simon thought with the ridiculous optimism that would never allow him to take disaster as seriously as he should, a temporary setback could already have brought them miraculously close to what after all had been their goal from the beginning.

"What . . ." Tammy began, but the Saint stopped her with a shake of his head.

He listened intently. The car sounded heavy, and its engine had a smooth expensive quietness, before it was switched off. A single door of the automobile opened and slammed hurriedly. The footsteps that spurned the gravel had a purposive male rhythm. There was no knock at the boathouse door, which opened, closed, and set off a babble of excited voices over which there suddenly rose a single incredulous infuriated shout:

"Here?"

The voice which uttered the almost despairing cry had a tantalisingly familiar tone, but Simon had no immediate chance to hear any more of it. The single word, like a lion trying to hurl itself out of a trap, was instantly smothered in a net of appeals and explanations. Although few other words were distinguishable, the tones and tempo failed somewhat to suggest a gathering of happy souls in harmonious relaxation.

Then the communicating door was flung open, and Captain Fowler himself strode in, with his cohorts crowding behind him.

It could have been nobody else. For he was the talkative Empire-builder whom Simon had met before dinner at the Golden Crescent, and the semi-familiarity of a voice which had puzzled the Saint a moment ago was explained.

"Well, well, well!" murmured the Saint. "What a surprise. But I suppose it shouldn't be, really. In most of the detective stories I've read, it's the most innocent-looking character who turns out to be the criminal mastermind. Only they usually don't unmask him until the very end."

"Dammit!" said Fowler. "What makes you think this isn't the end?"

His sandy hair was swept back as if by a recent typhoon, and his face was redder than ever. He had come to a halt a few feet in front of the Saint and Tammy, peering at them as if he had not really believed they could be there until he had seen them for himself. He clamped his jaws together and breathed noisily. Kalki came up beside him while Mahmud and Shortwave hovered in the comfortable obscurity of the background.

"For them, it must be," Kalki said.

"Thanks to a lot of stupid blundering," Fowler agreed angrily. He turned back to the Saint "Why did you have to get yourself into this, Templar? Who was bothering you?"

"I might ask you the same question," Simon countered. "Why aren't you off ruling the waves somewhere instead of picking on cooks and bottle-washers? Not a very noble pursuit for an officer and a gentleman."

"Ex-officer," Fowler reminded him.

"And ex-gentleman," the Saint concluded agreeably.

"I'd thrash you for that if you weren't tied," Fowler said.

"Then untie me," Simon suggested.

Fowler clenched his hands at his sides and turned to Kalki and his henchmen.

"You've all managed to botch this up beautifully!" he raged. "First that idiotic arm-breaking idea of Mahmud's, and then bollixing the car accident, and now bringing them here!"

"Don't forget, Fowler," Simon began, "the captain is always responsible—"

Fowler swung around to send a broadside at Kalki.

"Who told him my name?" he demanded furiously.

Kalki's tremendous chest expanded with hostility before he answered.

"It does not matter. We are going to kill him anyway."

"Yes. You've left us no choice, have you? Simple enough. Blabber everything to anybody we happen to run into. We can always kill them!"

Kalki's face became characteristically empurpled and his tiny eyes seemed to draw closer together.

"There is nothing else to say," he growled sulkily.

"Right, there isn't!" Fowler snapped. He looked down at the Saint again. "You wanted to say something? I may as well hear it."

"I was just going to remind you that you don't have all that excuse for playing Captain Bligh with your cronies here, because while they were arranging charades in the back room of the Golden Crescent you were loafing around chatting with me about current history."

"What else could I do?" Fowler said. He calmed down a little, behaving more like an officer enjoying a conversation with a captured equal—not unconscious of the fact that men of lower rank were listening. "I walked into the restaurant expecting to go through to the back to talk to my people, and there you were."

"Sometimes I'm starting to consider plastic surgery," said the Saint.

"I recognised you, of course," Fowler said, "and naturally I had no idea whether you were there by chance or by design."

"Well said, forsooth. 'By chance or by design.' You were born too late, Admiral. You have a lovely Victorian style."

Fowler looked uncomfortable, but went on.

"I assumed you knew nothing about me," he said, "but I had to find out what you did know, if anything." He turned his attention to Tammy for the first time. "Miss Rowan, I believe we've met only by telephone, and now that I've seen you in person I must say that I'm sorry we weren't able to become acquainted under different circumstances."

"You're the swine who rang up threatening to slash my face, I suppose," she said, with a defiance that surprised and impressed the Saint.

Fowler smiled and shrugged, his hands behind his back.

"I'm afraid so. You'll have to pardon my crudity at that time, but my experience in handling these things comes mostly from American films."

"I won't pardon anything," Tammy retorted. "Just untie us and let us out of here, or you'll be in real trouble."

Fowler reacted with a sigh and a quick fading of cordiality from his face.

"I am in real trouble," he said. "And so are you. It's unfortunate that only by putting you in much worse trouble can I save myself. I have a very valuable business going here—which I amply warned you not to interfere in. If either you or Mr Templar got out of this house it would be the end of my livelihood—not to mention me. Unless . . ." He studied Simon thoughtfully. "I should have thought that what I'm doing might have appealed to you, actually. Helping a lot of unfortunate people, even in a technically illegal way, into a better life—"

"And even into Paradise, via the old-world crucifixion route."

"That was only to make an example of an ungrateful traitor, even if it was rather crude."

"And to encourage the faithful to pay up promptly."

"From all I've heard," Fowler said irritably, "you've never been averse yourself to making a profit out of your so-called good deeds. Why do you suddenly have to be so righteous? Why do we have to be on opposite sides?"

"Because I never believed in blackmailing my so-called beneficiaries, just for one thing." The Saint shook his head. "No sale, Captain. If this is your idea of a proposition, I can only suggest that you try it as a suppository."

Fowler's thin lips compressed, and his florid complexion blanched momentarily, and then he shrugged.

"Too bad, old boy," he said, with a strained display of jauntiness. He turned to Kalki. "Well, that settles it. This is your mess. You get rid of it."

Tammy jumped to her feet, straining her wrists against the ropes that held them.

"You can't do that!" she cried. "You must be joking. We haven't done enough . . ."

Mahmud trotted forward anxious to assert himself, and pushed her back down into her chair.

"You have done enough," Fowler said coldly. "It's do-gooders like you, poking into things that are none of their business, that cause half the trouble in the world today. I must say I won't be sorry to see one less of you around after tonight."

"I can't believe they'd be stupid enough to really do it!" she exclaimed to the Saint, as if expecting him to arbitrate the dispute.

Fowler literally snorted, disdainfully, before Simon could answer. He spoke again to Kalki.

"Kill them—quietly—and put them in those two empty tar drums behind the house. Fill the drums up with wet cement. I'll have to pick them up and dump them offshore later."

"That's what I like," Simon said admiringly to Tammy. "The efficient executive type: quick decisions, no nonsense."

"Sorry to be so abrupt about it," Fowler said unsorrowfully. "I've got to make a pick-up tomorrow night and I've got no time to dilly-dally here."

"Still got the old sea-salt in the veins, hm?" Simon taunted. "What kind of scow are you using on the cross-Channel run?"

"That's none of your business."

"Doing your bit to sink England, though, aren't you?"

Fowler glared.

"That lot in the Admiralty didn't need me, and now as far as I'm concerned it's every man for himself."

"It's interesting," Simon philosophised. "I've almost never met a crook who couldn't make out a case that his particular racket wasn't only justified but society practically brought it on itself. The Sea Wolf here probably figures that if he can smuggle in enough illegal immigrants it'll help the Government to see the error of its ways and make them tighten up the immigration laws."

"I don't give a damn about the immigration laws," Tammy said irrationally. "I just think you'd better let us out of here."

Fowler glanced at his watch.

"That's wishful thinking, Miss Rowan, and I'm afraid I have to be a realist. I must go now. Good night."

Just before he reached the door, sweeping Shortwave and Mahmud out ahead of him, Kalki caught him deferentially by the arm and engaged him in a whispered conversation.

"No!" Fowler said impatiently. "The girl too! And just to be sure you don't get any fancy ideas, you drive the van ahead of my car so I can be sure we don't have any more slip-ups."

He made Kalki precede him through the door, and then followed him out without a backward look at the two people he had condemned to death.

"I think you've got an admirer," Simon said to Tammy. "I wonder if Kalki might take it into his head to rescue the princess from the dark tower."

Tammy's nerve had finally reached its limit. Her lips began to tremble even though she tried to control them.

"I'd rather be dead." She burst abruptly into a full flood of tears. "No, I wouldn't! I'm afraid! This is too horrible! I'm afraid to die!"

"Nature intended it that way," Simon said, with no flippancy in his tone.

"To die?" she sobbed.

"No, to dislike the idea of dying. And since I share your attitude, I suggest that we go to work at getting out of here."

"Out?" she moaned despairingly. "There isn't the slightest hope unless they change their minds."

She raised her bound wrists to dramatise her helplessness.

"Well," said the Saint, "at least your hands are tied in front of you. So you can see what you're doing if you want to come over and have a shot at untying me."

2

He rolled over away from the wall towards her, and she got up from the chair chattering half hysterically in the relief of realising that she was not utterly immobilised and that there might still be something that they could attempt, however desperate.

"I'll do my best—I will, honestly. Whatever you think, I didn't get my job on *The Evening Record* by being a completely scatterbrained female." She was on her knees beside him then, fumbling frantically. "I am trying, you know, but I can only use one hand at a time . . ."

"Take your time," Simon said coolly, trying to steady her. "And don't forget our secret weapon: that Girl Guide ring of yours. Even if you haven't got me untied, we might get Shortwave or Mahmud in here alone with us as some point. If the chance comes, use the ring and I'll use my feet."

"You make it sound so easy." She was almost giggling in the reaction of terror. "But what if the chance doesn't come?"

"Then we can try singing 'Swing Low, Sweet Chariot' in close harmony. Meanwhile, be sure your miniature Flit-gun is in firing order."

"There's nothing I can do to be sure without firing it," she told him. "All we can do is hope."

Simon did not have much confidence in the efficacy of wishful thinking, but for the moment there did not seem to be much else to count on.

The sounds of muttered words drifted in a meaningless jumble through the wall. Then the outside door opened and closed. After a minute the van rattled to life. Then the engine of Fowler's car caught smoothly. Gears were shifted, and both vehicles pulled away from the house and their mechanical voices quickly faded into the distance.

"The knots are so tight, and I can only use one hand at a time," Tammy whimpered. "I don't think I'm getting anywhere . . . Now I know what a sheep in a slaughterhouse feels like waiting to get his throat cut."

"Funny you should say that," said a voice like the scraping of a razor's edge on glass. "Real funny you should say that!"

Shortwave stood in the doorway, with the Saint's throwing knife in his hand, and Tammy started and gasped as his words answered hers.

To Simon, the little man's entrance was like a sudden chill wind in the room. He looked smaller than ever for some reason, a malevolent dwarf in workingman's clothes, his eyes red-rimmed and thirsty for blood. In his small hand the slender knife seemed the size of a Roman sword, but much more sinister. There was no guard to protect the hand of its wielder from an opponent's blows: the bare double edges were for attack only, the point for sudden and silent piercing.

As Shortwave stepped into the room, Mahmud appeared reluctantly behind him, but hung back at the door as Shortwave gloated over his captives.

"Who wants to be first?" the little man asked, with a taunting lilt in his voice. "Volunteers step forward." He chuckled. "Sorry, I forgot you can't step forward. How about crawling . . . like a worm?"

"I guess that's a thrill you don't get very often," Simon said.

But he said it quietly and steadily, without too much goading mockery that might trigger a sudden attack he could not hope to fend off. In fact, all the mockery that ordinarily danced like summer-light in his eyes had frozen into an ice-blue glint that brought the scrawny American up short when he saw it. The Saint's eyes were so coldly contemptuous that it would have been difficult for an observer to believe that he was the one with his hands and feet tied, while the other man held the knife.

Shortwave came forward and grabbed Tammy by one upper arm, yanking her to her feet with a show of brute strength that he could only have made with such a slight victim, and wrenched her back into the chair. He circled around to confirm that the ropes were still on Simon's wrists. Then, avoiding the Saint's uncanny eyes, which followed every move he made, turned to Mahmud.

"You waitin' to help?" he asked.

Mahmud showed distinct signs of being anything but ready to assist in surgery. He looked sick, and he moved his hands behind him to hide their agitated fluttering.

"I will mix the cement," he said. "Fowler told me—"

"I know," Shortwave said curtly. "So do it!"

Mahmud withdrew gratefully and a moment later opened and slammed the outer door. He had seemed in command when he and Shortwave had captured Simon and Tammy. Now it was as if some subtle transfer of power had wordlessly taken place from the leader who balked at anything more disagreeable than long-range killing and the subordinate who could enjoy the running of live blood.

Shortwave regarded his sacrificial lambs with satisfaction, and stepped towards Tammy. The girl involuntarily shrank back in her chair, twisting to one side in a futile attempt to get away from the point of the knife, which he took sadistic pleasure in bringing very slowly closer and closer to her face.

Simon's eyes were on the heavily wrought golden metal of her ring. Her hands, crossed in front of her and tied at the wrists, looked white and rigid. If she was really lapsing into a freeze of terror it could easily be too late before she used the tear-gas cartridge, if she ever used it at all.

"Wait!" he shouted.

Shortwave kept the knife a few inches from Tammy's face as he looked at the Saint.

"Anything wrong?" he asked. "Ladies first, right? We gotta be gentlemen, don't we?"

"Maybe we could make a deal," Simon said.

"You're a real wheeler and dealer, ain't you?" the little man said. "But not with me. You belted me one, remember? Seeing you squirm is the only deal I want."

Out of the corners of his eyes Simon caught a slight movement of Tammy's hands. His interruption had started the thaw in her terror that he had hoped it would. Her face was no longer a plaster mask of fear. She was looking past the freshly honed knife blade at Shortwave's face. He was still not quite within range, but she raised her wrists slightly, calculating the angle of the ring, holding it steady until Shortwave should lean closer to her.

Then he flicked the knife point teasingly at her nose without quite touching her, and stepped back three paces.

Tammy closed her eyes; her hands drooped like wilted leaves. Simon himself felt as if the blood pounding along his veins had suddenly coagulated and grown lead-heavy.

"So," said Shortwave, not seeing the significant disappointment that a more alert eye might have noted in his prisoners, "who's in a hurry?"

He turned the knife and took its point in his right hand, dandled it for a moment as he sized up the distance between him and Tammy, then raised it handle-up for throwing. The Saint tensed his muscles for a desperate roll across the floor towards Shortwave's legs that might at least make the knife miss its living target.

But Shortwave abruptly let the knife topple straight down from his fingers in a lazy somersault through the air and stick into the floor at his feet. Laughter whistled up through his uneven teeth. Tammy opened her eyes and glared at him with pure hatred.

"Why not let's have a little fun first?" he said.

He stepped up to her again, empty-handed—and cupped the empty hands on her breasts.

Tammy brought her own hands up, as if in the instinctive attempt to fend him off, but in a motion which at the same time brought them close to his face, directly under his nose. And in exactly that perfect moment and position, as if she had mastered it from a textbook, with a twist of a thumb and the clenching of a fist, she detonated the tear-gas cartridge straight into his face.

This time it worked. The sound of the discharge was negligible, but the effect was stupendous. As the gas puff blossomed into Shortwave's eyes he gave a startled screech and staggered back, bent almost double, rubbing his distorted countenance furiously.

The Saint, in the instant of the miniature explosion, also went into action, rolling across the floor like a log down a mountainside. It was an unorthodox means of locomotion, but it was the only way to get to Shortwave before he started to recover. The little man was still blind and choking, hunched over with his head almost level with his waist, when Simon arrived beside him. The trip had taken only two or three seconds, and the Saint decided that he had time for a more devastating attack than the rotary crash into Shortwave's shaky shins that he had first thought might be necessary. Without any pause, he stopped on his back, drew his knees almost to his chin—cocking his lithe body on to his shoulders—and unleashed a double-footed kick straight up into Shortwave's face.

It was an instantaneous uncoiling of supremely conditioned muscle that drew power from the whole magnificent length of the Saint's body, from shoulder blades to thighs, and concentrated its entire force in the heels of his shoes as they came into crunching contact with the forepart of Shortwave's steel-plated head. The would-be Jack the Ripper was rocketed straight up; then, with neither conscious will nor strength of limb to guide or support him, he crashed down like a dropped doll beside the Saint in a totally limp condition which the Saint only regretted might not prove permanent. But there was no doubt that he would be out of the game for a long time.

"Good girl!" Simon said softly. "I take back all my rude remarks about your little toy."

She was already out of her chair and on her knees by the knife Shortwave had teasingly let fall to the floor.

"You can send me a bouquet later," she said. "Here, I'll cut you loose."

She pulled the blade out of the wood while Simon scooted around into a sitting position with his back towards her.

"I'm glad we're good friends," he said as he felt the sharp edge of Anna bite into the cords an inch or so from his pulse.

"To the end," she muttered. "And this was almost it."

"It still will be if Mahmud comes in here before you've got me loose," he said. "But I don't think he will. Listen."

He turned his head slightly, and Tammy concentrated too, without letting up in her careful work behind him.

"He's mixing our concrete comforters," Simon said. "It'll keep him occupied for a while."

The ropes gave way. Shortwave was still motionless, bleeding quietly to himself. Simon turned quickly, took the knife from Tammy, and untied the ropes that held his ankles. Then he untied her hands, also without using the knife, and turned to search Shortwave for his gun.

At that moment the busy scraping outside stopped. Both the Saint and Tammy reacted as if the silence had been a sudden loud noise.

"Is he coming?" she breathed.

"I'll see. You take what's left of those ropes and tie up Shortwave. If you can find his gun, keep it handy—and use it if you have to!"

Simon was talking on the run. He kept Anna in his hand and hurried through the outer part of the boathouse and across to the side door.

The scraping of metal on wood started again. The Saint peeped cautiously out. The light from the cobwebbed window fell across Mahmud's heaving back as he worked with a hoe to mix cement in a low wooden trough on the ground in front of him. Beside him were bags of sand and lime, and a garden hose was squirting water into the straggly grass near his feet.

The Saint glanced around, saw no better weapon than he was holding already, and decided to move on Mahmud immediately while his back was turned and he was preoccupied with his work. He pushed the door wider, with tentative fingers, praying that the hinges would not squeak: they didn't.

About twenty feet away, Mahmud went on stirring the cement. Simon opened the door just enough to let himself through and slipped out. Mahmud could have noticed the variation in the light falling from behind him, but he did not.

Planting his feet very carefully, the Saint moved stealthily towards his prey; he still hadn't located the Pakistani's rifle, and had to reckon with the possibility that Mahmud might have put it down somewhere within easy reach.

When he was about ten feet away, Mahmud stopped pushing and pulling the hoe through the heavy mixture and straightened up to stretch his muscles. Simon froze. No stalking tiger could have attained a state of more absolute motionlessness. The only sounds for several seconds were Mahmud's laboured breathing and the quiver and squeak of branches overhead in the night wind.

Then it looked as if Mahmud was going back to stirring. He prodded the mixture, and apparently disapproved of its consistency. Holding the hoe with one hand, he turned and stooped to pick up the garden hose.

At that point he caught a glimpse of the legs of the man behind him, and it was his turn to freeze.

"What's for breakfast, chef?" the Saint asked genially. "Long pig in a blanket?"

Mahmud leapt up, almost falling back into the tank of cement he had made, and grabbed the hoe defensively in both hands. He was staring at the Saint with an incredulous horror that gripped even his vocal cords when he tried to shout for help.

"Shortwave!" he croaked. "He's out here! Shortwave! Quick!"

"Shortwave is more with the dead than the quick," Simon informed him. "Which would you rather be?"

Mahmud had already noticed the knife balanced all too comfortably in Simon's right hand, the direction of its point indicating that he, Mahmud, had been singled out for its undivided attention. He swept the hoe to one side and fanned it back and forth between himself and the Saint, not so much trying to attack as to keep Simon at bay.

"Shortwave?" he called shrilly, but no longer very hopefully.

"He won't be answering," the Saint assured him. "But if you'll answer a few questions, I'll consider not sinking your floating kidneys with this pig sticker. While you're pondering, let me remind you that people who shoot up other people's cars and try to kill them can't expect very friendly treatment unless they're willing to make amends."

The Pakistani's eyes telegraphed his next move, and before he could make a dash for the car parked around beside the house Simon took four sudden paces and cut off that path of escape.

"I'm warning you, Mahmud," Simon said more harshly, "unless you want your appendix removed by a rank amateur, you'd better drop that hoe and start telling me all about Fowler."

Mahmud cocked back the hoe and hurled it at the Saint. It came as no surprise, but even so Simon had to duck, dodge, and momentarily lose his balance in order to keep from getting hit. That gave Mahmud a chance to whirl and dive for something in the dark shadows where the garden hose joined the wall of the house. With a sinking heart Simon saw the long barrel of the rifle flash dully into the light as Mahmud jerked it to his shoulder. Simon's heart sank more for Mahmud than for himself: he had felt the Pakistani had been forced into the role of assassin and deserved something less than what Simon would instantly have to do to him in order to preserve the sanctity of his own skin.

There was no time for calculation. Few men on earth but the Saint could have thrown a knife with lethal accuracy in that light and in that split second of urgency. He scarcely had time even to move his arm. It was a throw from the wrist—the flick of a deadly dart with an almost imperceptible effortlessness at a dim slender target whose finger was even at the instant tightening on a trigger.

But the Saint's aim was so sure and his reflexes so swift that Mahmud's finger never even finished the short movement it would have had to complete in order to send a bullet smashing into Simon's chest. Instead, the knife found its target with the precision of a guided missile.

Mahmud gasped. First the rifle clattered to the ground, and then he fell beside it. By the time Simon got to him, the last embers of life had faded from his open eyes.

3

As the Saint walked back towards the room where he had been held prisoner, Tammy Rowan poked her head out.

"Is everything all right?" she asked.

"For us it is," he answered. "I had to kill Mahmud."

He said it as he reached her. She looked at him questioningly and saw from the simple directness of his eyes that he was doing no more than stating a fact.

"Good," she said firmly, and her knees uncooperatively gave way and she started to faint.

He caught her in his arms and held her until she got back her equilibrium. Holding her, for whatever reason, was an act that really merited a man's absolute attention, but even so the Saint could not help noticing that she had trussed up Shortwave with so many windings of rope that he would have looked completely at home in the Egyptian sarcophagus section of the British Museum.

"Oh, Simon, it was so horrible while you were gone! I imagined all sorts of awful things."

"Mahmud went for his rifle and I had to use my knife," he explained casually. "How's our friend here?"

"Oh, he's awful! He looks like a dead rat."

"Well, I suppose even that's some improvement over what he looked like before. Just so long as he's not really dead. He's our only easy way to finding out how to catch up with Kalki the Creep and Fowler." He moved Tammy a little away from him and had a physicianly look at her face. "Do you think you can navigate on your own power now?"

She looked at him uncertainly, with a warmth in her sea-green eyes that he had not seen beneath their businesslike intensity before.

"I'm not sure I want to," she said.

But before he could react she pulled away and walked over to Shortwave's prone form.

"I have a feeling he's not going to be answering any questions for quite a while, don't you?" she said.

"In that case we may as well settle down in this luxurious hideaway and pass the hours in cheerful dalliance and—"

She looked at him with incipient panic in her expression.

"Please, just get me out of here as fast as possible," she begged. "Otherwise I'll come down with the screaming heebie-jeebies. I really will! And anyway, somebody might come back."

"Not right away," the Saint said. "And where could we take our limp little friend without being importuned with offers from every taxidermist in the south of England? And just think of the scandal if he were found in your flat . . ."

"My flat?" she squealed.

"Yes. You could be up on fifty different charges: operating an illegal radio station, taking in lodgers without a licence, cruelty to animals—"

"Never mind the other forty-seven," she interrupted. "Because nobody's ever going to find him anywhere near where I live."

"Well, I'm not interested in entertaining him either. So let's see what the other accommodations are like in this riverside château."

The upstairs was no startling contrast, but it was an improvement. It did not suggest that Fowler himself spent his leisure hours there, but rather that it served as an occasional billet for such minions as Mahmud, Kalki, or Shortwave, who might be left in charge of even more transient guests. The furnishings were sparse and old and depressing, overlaid with stained lace and yellowed antimacassars; however, one of the two bedrooms seemed to have been unused since its linen was last changed, and there was a reasonably clean bathroom.

"We might do worse than stay here," Simon said. "For a while, anyway. Driving around in the middle of the night, we could always be unlucky enough to get stopped by a police patrol looking for somebody to try their Breathalyser on, and then Shortwave might be an embarrassment."

"But what if the others come back?" she asked.

"They weren't planning to, apparently, but if they do, so much the better. The last thing they'll be expecting to find is me with a rifle and Mahmud up to his scalp in instant quicksand."

"Delightful."

Simon countered her shudder with a cool shrug.

"You may find the idea easier to swallow if you'll recall that you and I would have been hamburger or roasted pigeon if your car had cracked up the way he wanted it to. Now why don't you curl up and rest a bit while I take care of Mahmud and stand the first watch. You can keep Shortwave's popgun for a comforter. When I'm finished outside I'll see that you're okay and then guard our little nest with my trusty blunderbuss. I hope Fowler or Kalki does come back. They'd save us a lot of chasing around."

Tammy brushed her blonde hair wearily away from her face.

"I'm exhausted, but I'll never sleep here," she complained. "On the other hand, how can you be sure you'll stay awake all night?"

"My strength is as the strength of ten because my heart is pure," Simon explained. "And the blood of Lancelot and Siegfried surges in my iron veins, reinforced by charms and talismans which make me impervious to all human weakness . . ." His eyes held hers for a moment. "Or almost all."

He went back downstairs, again checked the trussing of Shortwave, who still showed no signs of returning animation, and took off his coat and draped it over the back of a chair. Then he went outside and turned to the necessary job that was waiting for him.

When he had finished almost an hour had passed, and his shoulders ached a little from the unaccustomed effort of stirring wet cement and shovelling it into the two big metal drums. One of the drums took more cement, because Mahmud's body helped to fill up the other. In the second container the Saint put a partial stuffing of leafy twigs cut from nearby bushes, so as to make the weight of the two drums not too greatly different.

He left the two steel barrels brimming with concrete near the side door, where anybody arriving would see them right away and—assuming the arriver was in on the plot—think that Shortwave and Mahmud had done their jobs according to plan. He mentally ran over the current situation: Kalki and Fowler on their way to parts unknown, Fowler planning a "pick-up" at the end of the day which would presently be dawning, which undoubtedly meant the joyous arrival on England's shores of another misguided batch of reverse-order colonists. Meanwhile, a pair of minor pests had been taken out of circulation, one of them permanently, but the major miscreants still had their bill to pay—to which, Simon reflected, could fairly be added the write-off of Tammy Rowan's car.

He pondered his next move as he watched the branches of the big trees behind the boathouse quiver and flail in the wind against the barely perceptible luminescent background of the sky. Once more in his miracle-punctuated life he was standing with the good earth beneath his feet and sniffing the good air when by all acceptable guesses he ought to have shuffled off this mortal coil and—as the mystically minded might say—begun operations in another sphere. He savoured the sensation with the quiet gratitude of a man who has come to accept marvels as a part of his everyday experience without ever losing his respectful appreciation of them.

But while one such escape would have been more than enough in the life of most men, Simon Templar was already thinking of courses of action that would more than likely bring him face to face with death again within twenty-four hours. He could not afford to waste time. Men like Fowler, who apparently took care of the nautical end of the immigration game, were not likely to continue their normal routine once persistent investigators started showing up in upsetting numbers. If the Saint was not able to trace Fowler and Kalki before this same time tomorrow, a lot more sunrises might follow before he was able to pick up their trail again.

Shortwave knew where Fowler would be during the crucial day that was now on its way towards dawning, so it was to Shortwave's health and immediate future that Simon turned his consideration.

He picked up Mahmud's Winchester, which he had already emptied, tested, and reloaded for use in case he had been interrupted during his work, and went back into the boathouse.

The scrawny killer lay as still as ever in his windings of secondhand rope. The Saint began to fear that his two-legged kick might have had fatal consequences, which would undoubtedly have brought satisfaction to the grim gods of justice, but not to anybody wanting to dredge Shortwave's transistor brain for information.

A brief medical examination told Simon that the worst his charge could be suffering was concussion, accompanied by minor modifications of the facial profile which could be nothing but an improvement. But he had no way to tell how much longer the coma might last, so Simon gagged him with his own handkerchief and necktie and went to look for Tammy.

He found her in the upstairs living room, asleep in one of those bulbous overstuffed shorthaired chairs that looks as if it had been grown in a cellar along with mushrooms. Her position hinted at exhausted collapse in spite of her assertion that sleep would be impossible.

Simon tried not to disturb her while he moved quietly about the place, checking the drawers of a cabinet and a writing table for any useful information. He found nothing more enlightening than a spider or two and a few ancient and much-thumbed girlie magazines. The rest of the apartment was no more rewarding. The kitchen shelves were stocked with only a can of beans and a can of sardines, and the antique refrigerator offered nothing more nourishing than a bottle of beer. If the flat served as a meeting place for Fowler and associates, it apparently was not regularly inhabited.

Only mildly disappointed and not much surprised by his lack of success, the Saint turned out all the lights and sat down by the window, and watched till the sky began to pale, while Tammy breathed heavily near by. He had made up his mind to rest and relax without dozing off, and his reserves of fitness and strength and mental energy were so great that when he stood up again he was able to confront the day with as much alertness and enthusiasm as he could have garnered from six hours' sleep.

After a visit to the bathroom, he came back and spoke gently to Tammy.

"Time to get up."

She groaned and tried to burrow farther down into the cushions. He jigged her shoulder.

"You've just been made editor of *The Evening Record*, and Kalki has offered to divorce Fowler and marry you."

Her eyes opened slightly and she suddenly jerked upright.

"Oh! What's happening? I fell asleep!"

"Rose-fingered dawn is about to glide through the fields and glens," Simon said, "and we want to beat the morning traffic rush into London."

He took her hand and helped her to her feet. Her cheek was creased lightly from contact with the chair, her hair was in platinum tangles, and her eyes were puffy from sleep. As she stood up she saw her face in a mottled mirror over the fireplace.

"Oh, I look awful!"

"Only the least bit ghastly," he concurred encouragingly. "Go and see what you can do to repair the damage while I see if Shortwave is still snoring."

Still holding one hand to her face, she wobbled to the door and glanced back.

"I didn't mean to go to sleep," she said. "Did anything happen?"

"Nothing you don't know about already."

"What's going to happen?"

"We'll talk about that on the road, shall we? I'd just as soon not stick around this house any longer than we have to now that it's light."

"Amen!" she said, and hurried out.

The Saint went downstairs to where he had left Shortwave tied and gagged. Because of the small filthy window panes, that room was still almost as dark as night. Simon skirted the human bundle on the floor, and threw open the side door, letting in some of the dim morning light. When he turned, he saw that Shortwave was no longer comatose but wide awake, staring up with glistening eyes, wriggling in his bonds like a netted fish.

"Good morning, Sunshine!" the Saint said to him cheerily. "I hope you had lovely nightmares."

Shortwave could not say anything because of the handkerchief in his mouth, but he made incoherent and clearly unhappy sounds.

Simon gazed down at him benevolently. Using only one hand, he moved the rifle he carried from the casual angle at which he had allowed it to hang and placed its cold muzzle against Shortwave's forehead directly between the eyes.

"Take a long look, chum," he said, with the most ghoulish intonation he could command with a straight face. "Because when I start asking you to recite your lessons, and if you forget anything important, the zero I give for flunking is going to drill straight through your tin-plated head . . ."

4

"But what are we going to do with him?" Tammy asked. "We might have been able to sneak him into one of our flats at night, but now we'd never get away with it."

She referred to Shortwave, who was now neatly tucked away in the trunk of the late Mahmud's car. Simon, at the wheel, had left the boathouse behind and was feeling his way from one crossroads to the next on his way to the main London highway.

"It's just as well we can't sneak him into one of our flats," he said. "He's not the kind of house guest I'd enjoy anyway."

"What can we do with him, then?"

She had been tensing visibly whenever some work-bound driver came into view in his dew-covered automobile, as if each car might harbour a whole troop of detectives specifically charged with rooting Shortwave out from under a blanket in the boot of a late-model Ford.

"We can do the same sort of things to him that he was going to do to us," the Saint said nonchalantly. "Or at any rate we can threaten to. Until we get what we want out of him."

"I'm starting to wish I'd stuck to plain reporting," Tammy said. "Let's just give ourselves and him up to the police."

"Why should we give ourselves up to anybody?" the Saint asked. "We haven't done anything wicked yet."

Tammy looked at his innocent profile with surprise in her wide eyes, like one child witnessing another in some undreamed-of audacity. In the few minutes it had taken them to prepare to leave the boathouse the ravages of the strenuous night had disappeared from her face, leaving her as fresh as the approaching dawn.

"But back there," she began, "you . . ."

Simon raised one finger to his lips.

"See no evil, speak no evil," he said. "I have an excellent memory, and all I can remember about that place is that we were kidnapped and left there tied up, possibly to be murdered later, but we managed to untie ourselves and escape, because they were too silly to leave anyone to guard us. Isn't that approximately what you remember?"

She sat back and shook her head. There was the suspicion of a smile on her lightly reddened lips.

"Approximately," she murmured.

The Saint glanced at her with deep aesthetic appreciation.

"So," he said, "we don't have anything to give ourselves up for, do we? Our object, in fact, is to keep ourselves free and mobile so that we can track down Kalki the Corn-ball and his nautical buddy, and get your exclusive story. We aren't going to the police yet because that would put all the other newspapers on the trail."

"Lovely," she said. "Except we don't have the faintest idea where they are."

"We will," Simon replied, "as soon as we've had a heart-to-heart chat with our little friend in the trunk. We already know Fowler is making some kind of pick-up tonight, and I don't think he means in Shepherd Market."

Tammy gave a despairing sigh.

"Then we should have waited somewhere where we could watch the boathouse. You already guessed that he was planning to bring his immigrants there."

"'Planning' is the operative word. From the look of the place, it's still being prepared for that. Fowler mightn't be planning to inaugurate it today. You could see, it's still being worked on. And after last night, he might even feel more like postponing the grand opening. So we can't afford to take the chance. Since it's a fair bet that he'll still use another old-established landing place tonight, I'd rather try to catch him even farther up the line. And that's where fate allows Shortwave his moment of glory. Against a Wagnerian background transmitted direct to him from Radio Three, he will sing for us at the top of his miserable little lungs, in the course of which concert we shall learn just exactly where Commander Fowler is running his moonlight cruise this evening."

They had finally come to a highway which a signpost identified as the A40, and Simon swung the car eastwards towards London. The misty pearl-grey of the sky was still barely tinged with pink, and the roads were almost deserted in the hush between the tardiest stragglers and the front-runners of the matutinal deluge.

"So," he continued, "we'll take Shortwave to a cosy spot where he can warm up for his command performance, and then I'll be on my way to foul up Captain Fowler."

"We'll be on our way," she corrected. "Don't forget our bargain."

"Sorry," he said. "My memory is perfect but a bit selective."

"So I gathered," she said. "You've almost forgotten to tell me where this cosy spot is where we're taking Shortwave."

"The Golden Crescent," Simon answered.

She stared at him.

"That restaurant? Why there?"

"Because neither of us wants him home, so that was the best place I could think of to park him. Do you know the owner?"

"I've seen him when I was poking around looking for leads on my story, that's all."

The Saint accelerated around a lumbering truck which was already making a heroic start on polluting the atmosphere of the new-borning day with the abominable fumes of the unlamentable Herr Rudolf Diesel's contribution to the horrors of the internal combustion engine.

"Well," he continued, "Mr Haroon's role in this immigrant game isn't completely clear to me, and I'd like to get it straight. Obviously Fowler and his friends have felt chummy enough with Haroon to make his restaurant a meeting place—"

"But Kalki said Haroon wasn't part of the gang," Tammy interrupted.

"Right. Which I could believe. On the other hand, they must have him pretty well under their thumbs, or they couldn't risk working as close to him as they have."

On the almost deserted roads, their speed was limited by practically nothing but his discretion, and in what seemed no time at all they were running into Kensington.

"They've probably just got him scared to death the way they have everybody else," Tammy said.

"Probably," Simon agreed. "I wouldn't guess that our fat friendly restaurateur is the bravest or strongest man in the world. He's got an imbalance of blubber over moral fibre. If we need him on the side of the angels, we'll just have to scare him worse than the bad guys did. But we can't afford to have an uncertain factor rattling around in the works at this stage, and Mr Haroon is certainly an uncertain factor, so we'll drop in for breakfast with Shortwave and see what we can do about battening them both down."

"He won't be open this early."

"We could hardly do this during business hours—that's why we had to wait out most of the night at that boathouse. But he lives right above the restaurant," Simon told her. "He'll probably still be in bed counting cheap sheep jumping into his saucepans."

When they arrived at the alley behind the Golden Crescent, it was just after six o'clock. The city was barely coming to life, outside of the meat and produce market districts; and in this area dominated by restaurants and theatres, their doors all closed, there was still more an atmosphere of sleeping off the night before than of getting ready for a new day's business. The few pedestrians seemed on their way to somewhere else, and in the alley there was no sign of life at all.

Simon pulled up at the back door of Haroon's establishment and switched off the car's engine.

"Have you ever been to his flat?" Tammy asked.

"No, but he once showed me a separate door around on the street in front. You wait here while I go rouse him and have him open this entrance."

"You're not supposed to go anywhere without me," she said.

The Saint looked momentarily tired.

"I seem to remember that you said that before. Surely we can be parted for three or four minutes without your hurling yourself off Lovers' Leap."

"Do you promise you won't try to give me the slip?" she asked earnestly.

"I do so swear," he said. "I won't be gone any longer than it takes to pump up Abdul for the day and roll him down the stairs. All right?"

"All right," she said. "But I still don't see why I have to stay here." She looked over behind her seat. "He certainly can't get away."

"That's what he would have said about us at one point last night," the Saint reminded her. "But let's also hope that he hasn't suffocated by this time. If he has, it might solve Abdul's meat problem, but it won't help us."

He avoided any more discussion by getting quickly out of the car and walking down to the alley's mouth and around to the front of the restaurant. Next to it was an open doorway exposing worn wooden stairs which led to rooms above the street level. The staircase was dark and smelled sour, like old beer. At the top, to the left and right, Simon found a choice of two doors. The one on the right bore a thumbtacked card signed "Evans" and the one to the left was unmarked.

The Saint knocked on the left-hand door. Presently there was a scuffling sound from within, and then silence. Simon rapped on the door again. More silence.

"Abdul," he called softly. "This is Simon Templar."

Reluctant footsteps approached the door.

"Mr Templar?" Haroon's voice asked. "It is you, is it?"

"Yes, it is."

"What do you want?"

"Are you always this friendly with big-spending customers?" the Saint enquired. "Among other things, I want to help your business."

A key rattled in the lock and the door opened a fraction.

Then it opened fully and revealed Abdul Haroon in leather slippers, dark trousers, and clean open-collared white shirt. He looked freshly scrubbed and shaven, like a Grade A apple.

"I don't want any trouble with anybody," he said hastily, holding one plump hand out as if he might try to fend off the Saint if he tried to cross the threshold.

"You won't have any if you're a good fellow and help me," Simon told him pleasantly. "As I understand the situation, you've had a little trouble making up your mind just whose side you're on in this business of Kalki's and Fowler's, and it's about time—"

Haroon's shiny round face suddenly stretched into a great tremulous pudding of dismay.

"What are you talking about?" he gasped. "I don't know anything about it!"

He started to close the door, but before he could do it the Saint pushed into the room.

"Then you'd better listen," he said. "I know all about Kalki and Fowler and Shortwave now—and also about Mahmud's fake broken arm. Incidentally, this wasn't Mahmud's lucky day. You'll have to start looking for a new waiter."

Haroon was shaking his head violently, as if to convince the world and the gods that he was not really there and not really hearing anything at all. He closed the door at the mention of Mahmud's name, though, to shut himself and the Saint off from any prying ears outside the flat.

"Mahmud?" he mumbled. "What happened to him?"

"He's booked for a long sea voyage," said Simon. "But more to the point is your future, which is not going to be terribly rosy if you can't explain to me and the police why you've been letting Kalki and Fowler use your beanery as a clubhouse."

Haroon wrung his bejewelled hands, creating the clear impression that at any moment he might fall to his knees and dissolve in tears.

"I didn't do anything!" he protested frantically. "They made me. They would have killed me if I'd told anybody or tried to stop them!"

"I'm inclined to believe you," Simon admitted. "So do you propose to repent now and help me nail those creeps or shall we take a ride to Scotland Yard?"

Haroon looked less actively distraught and more despairing.

"You work for the police?" he asked.

"No, but I don't mind giving them a helping hand when it suits me. Which way would you like it?"

Haroon's hands dropped limply to his widely separated sides like a pair of discarded rubber toys.

"What do you want me to do?" he asked weakly.

Simon smiled and put a hand on the other man's shoulder—a touch which became a firm grip as he steered Haroon out of the door and on to the stairs.

"I don't want you to do anything that you're not already good at. I have a very thin friend downstairs and I want you to help fatten him up. After that you can start preparing a feast to celebrate our final victory over Kalki the Conquered and Fowler the Foundered."

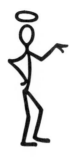

CHAPTER FIVE:

HOW SHORTWAVE ENJOYED HIS BREAKFAST, AND THE SAINT USED A CONVENIENT CELLAR

1

Abdul Haroon preceded the Saint down the stairs to the street like an unwilling hippo.

"I've parked in back," the Saint told him. "My friend is a bit shy."

"I carry only the key to the front," Haroon replied. "We can go through."

He walked the few feet to the main door of his restaurant flinging quick glances into the street and over his shoulder as if he were a fat schoolboy sneaking into a forbidden pantry.

"What are you so worried about?" Simon asked. "None of the baddies knows I'm here—and anyway, I'll protect you if you prove to deserve it."

Haroon bent stiffly forward and unlocked the glass door so amply identified in gilt lettering as the portal of the Golden Crescent.

"You cannot know what a torment my life has been since these people began to interfere in things and threaten me," he said in a low voice. "But what could I do? You have seen how they treat people who do not co-operate. Come in, come in . . ."

He held the door open and closed it quickly behind him as soon as the Saint had entered. The restaurant was dim because of the thick colourless curtains that had been drawn across the plate-glass windows. Haroon threw the bolt, and the shade which covered the door swayed a few times, sending a wing of sunlight fluttering across the wall before the room settled into a kind of undersea gloom again.

"But it's only people who don't co-operate who ever stop rats like Kalki and Fowler," Simon said. "On the other hand, as I'm sure you must have said to yourself, who wants to be a dead hero? How much did they pay you?"

Abdul Haroon's eyes grew extraordinarily round and whitely large.

"They paid me nothing! They paid me nothing! They threatened to frighten away my customers . . . to kill me! Ali tried to go against them and you know what happened to him!"

"All right, calm down," the Saint said in a not especially soothing voice. "Let's go on back."

Haroon stalled when he reached the passageway which led through from the dining room to the kitchen.

"But you haven't told me anything," he protested. "Who is there? What do you want with me?"

"I've told you: I have an undernourished friend, and a good dose of your curry will do him worlds of good. Let's go bring him in."

Simon prodded Haroon's overflowing waistline with a stiff finger, which set him in motion again through the kitchen and into the back room where Mahmud had writhed on the floor in mock agony the night before. It was dark because there were no windows, until Haroon switched on a light, and the place smelled as fragrant of spices as it had the first time Simon had entered it. The perfumes of exotic gastronomy had an ineradicable way of permeating the premises of their preparation around and beyond all human tumult.

"Open up," Simon insisted, and Haroon finally fumbled a large key from a nail on the wall and unfastened the back door with it.

The Pakistani blinked at the morning sunlight, and then blinked again with shock as he seemingly recognised the car which was parked outside.

"Where did you get that?" he blurted.

"All things will be revealed to you in the day of their ripeness," the Saint said poetically. "I suppose you could classify this little buggy as the spoils of war."

He left Haroon gaping from the doorway and opened the car to greet a highly relieved Tammy Rowan. She caught his hands and let herself be helped out of the car.

"I'm so glad to see you!" she gasped. "He was starting to thump around back there something frightful . . ." She stared dubiously at the bulky form of Abdul Haroon for the first time. "Oh . . ."

"This is our ally, at least for the moment," the Saint said. "Mr Haroon meet Mademoiselle X."

Haroon automatically half-formed a smile before abandoning the effort for a sickly droop.

"I have met the lady," he said disconsolately. "She writes for a newspaper."

"But she isn't the special guest I was referring to," the Saint went on with unflappable good cheer. "Would you mind lending your useful waistline to block the view from the end of the alley while I unload the guest of honour. Tammy, you could add your own svelte silhouette over there, just in case any early bird waddles by with his eyes open enough to notice anything."

Tammy Rowan complied with the most pleasing competence, and herself shoved Haroon into quivering co-operation, while Simon opened the trunk of the car.

"What is it?" Haroon croaked, seeing the blanket-covered shape.

The Saint grabbed Shortwave's feet and pulled him half out of the car. The ex-jockey's scuffed brown shoes were all of him that showed from underneath the covering.

"You might ask 'who is it,'" Simon said, "but on second thought 'what' probably is more appropriate. How about lending me a hand."

Haroon, feet attached by some invisible force to the threshold, tried to flap the whole situation away with both hands.

"A dead man?" he twittered. "A body? In heaven's name, take it away!"

"It's not dead yet," Simon said. "Observe."

He kicked one of Shortwave's invisible shins, bringing forth a definitely animate squawk from the opposite end of the blanket.

"No, no!" Haroon cried. "I have nothing to do with this. I'm only a poor man trying to—"

"Trying to straddle the fence till he sees which side is safest to jump on." The Saint's arm suddenly shot out and his fingers encircled one of Haroon's wrists like steel clamps and rearranged him in screening position. "So let's get it straight, Humpty Dumpty," he said, firing the words at point blank range into the fat man's frightened face. "You're going to jump on to my side or you're going to have a great fall that'll splash you halfway across Leicester Square. Now stand still while I lug in this new delicacy for your menu."

Abdul Haroon stood back while Simon lifted the blanket-swaddled shape effortlessly under one arm and carted it through the back door, and then followed with an alacrity that would have made a gazelle stare with admiration. He grabbed Shortwave's ankles, which happened to be colourfully adorned with bright purple socks, and took off in reverse while Tammy ran after them.

"Whoa!" Simon said when they were halfway through the kitchen, and ungently dropped his major share of the load. "Let's stop and unwrap him. Lock that door, please, Tammy."

While she was taking care of the outside door the Saint pulled the blanket off Shortwave, so that Haroon was able to identify him for the first time and gave a memorable imitation of a man discovering a scorpion in his cornflakes.

"Take him away!" he finally managed to gasp.

"I'm afraid he's yours to have and to hold for the duration, Abdul," the Saint said.

Shortwave's venomous eyes darted from Simon's to Haroon's face, Haroon avoided meeting them with his own almost tearful orbs.

"The duration?" he quavered.

"The duration of this little caper—until I've got Shortwave's friends bundled up as comfortably as he is." Simon looked down at his robe-swathed captive. His tone changed to one of reasonable persuasion. "And now, Shortwave, I want you to cleanse your black little soul a bit by telling us exactly what your friends Kalki and Fowler will be up to this evening—and exactly where. I'm going to take the gag out of your mouth and let the truth flow unimpeded into our grateful ears."

He stooped down and with one hand jerked the knot out of the necktie and whipped it and the handkerchief from between Shortwave's teeth.

Shortwave then delivered himself of a single terse phrase which turned Tammy's cheeks red and made coarsely clear his total disinterest in co-operating with the Saint.

"In that case," Simon said, imperturbably, "we'll have to try to win your heart through kindness." He straightened up. "Do you like curry?"

"No," snarled Shortwave.

"Good," the Saint rejoined genially. "Abdul, how about warming up a nice mess of your native pottage for our guest?"

Haroon looked at him uncomprehendingly.

"I do not understand."

"I want you to make some curry for Shortwave so hot that it will sear the soot off his insides, to borrow a figure of speech from his boss. I want you to concoct something so impeccably fiery that his tongue will thaw and babble like a mountain stream. I'm sure you have some leftovers we can fix up especially for the occasion?"

Haroon turned up his palms, turned down the corners of his mouth, and nodded. He was already on his way to the refrigerator when he thought again and stopped.

"Everything is made fresh every day," he claimed.

"I'm sure you could violate your high standards as a special favour to our friend. There must be a few tidbits lying around from last night."

Haroon turned expressionlessly to the refrigerator, opened it, and brought out a large metal pot which he set on the stove. He lifted the lid and looked inside.

"Lime-pickle sauce," he said.

"But probably not curried enough for Shortwave's taste," Simon said. "He likes it absolutely molten."

"I hate it," Shortwave said.

"Then you won't quibble about the seasoning, will you?" said the Saint. "Bring on the curry powder, Abdul. Bring on the red pepper. We're going to give this prodigal son a welcome he'll never forget."

2

While the sauce bubbled on the stove, Abdul Haroon ladled into it a number of tablespoons of chili powder and cayenne. Even he, with his cultural tolerance for culinary pyrotechnics, looked somewhat appalled at what he had wrought.

"Enough extra?" he asked.

"Let's not be miserly," Simon said. "Here."

He took down a bottle of tabasco sauce from one of the shelves and dumped its entire remaining contents into the simmering stew. Haroon looked at the empty bottle and at the concoction in the pan and then said something which the Saint found charming in its hushed simplicity:

"That will be very hot."

"Yes it will," Simon agreed. "If you remember the recipe, it might make you a new reputation."

He bent over Shortwave, caught some of the loops of rope which held him, and lifted him to a standing position. "Now come along, Marconi, and prepare to have your tongue loosened."

"You'll have to untie my feet," Shortwave said.

He was still playing the defiant little tough guy, a role he would have had to be fairly good in to survive in the circles he frequented. The Saint had felt sure he was not the type to cave in and start squealing his head off at the first threat of pressure. He was no Rock of Gibraltar, but he had probably taken enough punishment before in his life not to stand in awe of it, and his natural inclination to keep his trap shut would be reinforced by the fear of Kalki and Fowler that everybody who came into contact with the organisation developed very quickly.

The Saint hoped that some exotic and unexpected form of persuasion might have a more telling effect than conventional threats of death. Although Simon had always given wide latitude to his personal interpretation of the justification of means by ends, he was not an adherent of the thumbscrew and hot-iron school of winning friends.

The use of fists or more unpleasant implements on a man whose hands were tied was not in his repertoire.

"If you can't walk, hop," he told Shortwave, and pulled him towards the dining room.

Shortwave bounding along beside him like a one-legged kangaroo until they reached the first of the ghostly white tables in the semi-light of the public eating room.

"Sit," Simon said.

He shoved Shortwave into a chair and arranged him in a more or less orthodox sitting position when he threatened to topple on to the floor.

"What are you gonna d-d-d-d-do?" Shortwave asked.

"It's what you're going to do that's important," the Saint replied. "You're going to sing for your breakfast. I want to know how I can find Kalki and Fowler."

"I d-d-d-dunno," said Shortwave. "They d-d-d-d-on't tell me nothing."

He tried to sound unconcerned, as if such matters as the whereabouts of his bosses were so far from his ken that it had never even occurred to him to think of the question before. The Saint bent down, and the dangerous cobalt brightness of his eyes sliced through the other man's forced bravado.

"Listen, you humanoid short circuit," he said. "I know that you know where Fowler is operating his transport service tonight, and you're going to tell me, and you're going to get it right."

Shortwave blinked rapidly.

"I told you I d-dunno," he said with a little less conviction.

Simon straightened up to his full height and put his hands on his hips.

"Then you'd better get your antenna up and tune in fast," he said, "because you're going to tell me while I've still got time to drive there."

Tammy came in from the kitchen.

"Mr Haroon wants to know if you want rice too," she said.

"How about it, Shortwave?" Simon asked considerately. "Would you like rice?"

"I wouldn't like nothing."

"Clear enough," the Saint said. "A real purist. Coming up—one large order of Curry Vesuvius."

Abdul Haroon appeared in the dining room with a steaming bowl on a tray. He set it down in front of Shortwave, whose face twitched as the corrosive fragrance of the rusty yellow-green substance rose to his defenceless nostrils.

"No rice?" Haroon asked. "Chutney?"

"Nothing to dilute the full impact," Simon insisted. "You see, the customer is already starting to shed tears of joy at the mere prospect of sampling your cooking. Open wide, friend."

Shortwave sat with his skinny jaws clamped shut.

"You'll open up or we'll pry your mouth open with a cleaver. I assure you I can think of a lot worse things than this to do to you . . .

some of them inspired by you last night. So open up and either start talking or start chewing."

He dipped a spoon into the bowl and held it in front of Shortwave's mouth, which still did not budge.

"All right, Abdul," the Saint said. "Go get those hot tongs."

Shortwave opened his mouth and instantly Simon introduced the spoon and its contents. When he had withdrawn the empty spoon he held it threateningly just beyond Shortwave's lips.

"Now swallow like a nice boy," he said.

Abdul Haroon's lamb curry, in the state it ordinarily reached his patrons, was of that not quite unbearable degree of spicy hotness which a curry must have if it is to be a real curry and yet not irrevocably cauterise the taste buds. It brought happy moisture to the eyes, perspiration to the brow, and to the palate an addictive desire for more. Few were the European partakers of the dish who did not intersperse their bites with copious use of their handkerchiefs and with large profitable gulps of Haroon's wine and beer. Gratified, satisfied, half-melted, they would complete the meal with a sense of victory and the appearance of one who has walked through a Turkish bath fully clothed.

That was the curry ordinaire of the Golden Crescent. Shortwave had just been presented with a sauce so loaded with ardent powders of seeds, pods, and leaves as to make the normal torrid dish seem as bland as a bowl of scrambled eggs.

First Shortwave's skull-like face underwent a general horrified transformation, as a wax mask might change on sudden exposure to searing heat. His eyes opened wide. His crew-cut brown hair, already on end, seemed to bristle like the protective armament of an aroused porcupine. Then tears flooded from his eyes and he crumbled into a violent fit of coughing.

"I'd say it's a hit," the Saint said, looking up at Haroon and Tammy.

Tammy was in a state of empathetic numbness, but Haroon, after his first intense observation of the phenomenon, broke into a delighted grin.

"Ha, ha," he said, as precisely as if he were pronouncing the words from a grammar book. The laugh grew on him. "Ha-ha-ha-ha-ha!"

Suddenly he saw how Shortwave was glowering up at him, and the laugh caught in his throat and the grin was instantly withdrawn from his lips.

"Don't worry, Abdul," the Saint said. "Your days of being bullied by these rats are over. Right, Shortwave? Where are Fowler and Kalki?"

"I told you I dunno!" Shortwave said defiantly.

"You forgot to stutter—or maybe it's the curry cure," the Saint remarked. "Obviously what you need is more of the same."

Shortwave protested violently against the next heaping spoonful of curry before giving in and taking it. There followed the immediate question whether he was consuming it or being consumed by it. His appreciation this time was even more spectacular than the first. His whole body seemed ready to glow, and after the initial paroxysms he continued to gasp for air like an overtaxed steam engine. The Saint already had another mouthful ready for him, and in the concluding phases of his reaction to that Shortwave shook his head in what appeared to be surrender.

"Okay, okay," he finally rasped. "That's enough."

"If you have any doubts, there's plenty more where that came from," said Simon. His voice became deadly earnest. "And if this kind of treatment seems namby-pamby to you, I'm sure you do understand we can become a lot more inventive, especially since we don't have all day to soften you up."

Shortwave was looking genuinely defeated.

"They'll kill me if I tell," he said.

"We'll do worse if you don't."

Shortwave could think of no answer to that.

"What'll you do if I do tell?" he asked.

"If I were in your seat I'd concentrate on what'll happen if you don't start telling fast—but just to set things straight I'll tell you what we'll do. We'll keep you alive and in one piece, tucked away somewhere so we can really work you over if we find out you've given us the wrong information."

"But sometimes Fowler makes a plan and changes it," Shortwave said hastily. "What if I told you what I know and he changed his mind? Then you'd think . . ."

"Never mind what we'd think. What is the plan?"

Shortwave sat back in his chair, putting as much space as possible between his gullet and what was left of the curry. He took a deep breath.

"Fowler's got this cabin cruiser that he runs these wogs in on, and he moves it up and d-down the coast between jobs so nobody gets wise. What he uses is one of these . . ." Shortwave stopped. "He'll kill me if I tell you."

"I think I'd better have a word with your personal chef," the Saint said, looking around towards Abdul Haroon, who was watching from the other side of the room.

"I'd rather eat that stuff than what Fowler would do to me," Shortwave averred hopelessly.

"I wasn't thinking of fattening you up any more for the slaughter," Simon told. "I was just considering how you might do in a curry yourself. Abdul, how about bringing in a butcher knife and a long fork?"

"Seriously?" Abdul asked.

"Very seriously," said the Saint.

The glint in his eyes would have outdone the sharpness of the best-honed steel blade in Abdul's culinary arsenal. Shortwave did not wait to find out just how serious the Saint was.

"Okay," he said. "Just don't tell him I told you. It's one of them forts they sunk out in the water in the war. You know what I mean?"

"In the Thames Estuary?" the Saint asked him.

"Right."

"If they sunk it, how can Fowler use it?" Tammy asked.

"They were big things they floated out into the estuary and sank to use as anti-aircraft emplacements," the Saint explained. "The top part sticks up above the water. I've never seen one, unfortunately."

"Oh, I know," Tammy said. "And people tried to use them as pirate radio stations because they were outside the three-mile limit."

"And now they're abandoned," Simon said. "Or they were supposed to be. Which one does Fowler use—and what does he use it for?"

"The guys who bring the load over from the Continent stow them there and Fowler picks them up," Shortwave said.

He tried to describe the location of the unused fort which Fowler used.

"Who brings them over to the fort?" Simon asked.

"I d-d-dunno. He never comes and stays. He's just the one that runs loads over here for Fowler to pick up. These Indian guys wait on the fort for Fowler to run them in at night."

"And where does he run them in?"

"I couldn't tell you. Sometimes it's one place and sometimes it's another. There's plenty of places where nobody could see them coming in at night."

The Saint looked at Tammy.

"Does that sound like the truth to you?"

"What good's it to me to make it up?" Shortwave said. "Like you said, if I lie you come back and mess me up good."

"All right then," Simon said. "Tell me exactly how to find this fort—and I mean exactly."

For the next five minutes Shortwave gave instructions for locating the fort. It was less than five miles offshore, and it was lucky for the Saint that it was no farther, since Shortwave's direct experience with it was limited to two trips, and since his talent for observation and navigation left quite a lot to be desired.

"I can't help it," he finally said wearily. "That's all I know. You can find it. It ain't that hard."

"What time does he pick them up?" Simon asked. "Does he stay out there on the fort during the day?"

"I think he goes out in the afternoon and then comes in with the load after dark."

"What sort of boat does he have?"

"Some kind of cabin cruiser. Not too big." Obviously Shortwave was no boating buff. "Sometimes he keeps it at a yacht club down towards Southend."

"What's it called?"

"I dunno."

"For somebody with his own private built-in communications system there sure is a lot you 'dunno,'" the Saint said.

Shortwave's eyes rolled briefly up as if to inspect the top of his own head.

"I think you broke it," he said. "Since you kicked me I ain't heard nothing."

"That would be a pity," the Saint commiserated. "However, if your directions turn out to be helpful, maybe I'll reward you by having you wired for cassettes."

He looked at his watch and stepped away from the table, touching Tammy's arm to signal her to follow him. They walked alone back into the hall.

"What do you think?" she asked.

"I think it's all we've got to go on. It's even possible he is telling the truth. I think we threw a pretty good scare into him."

"So we go to the fort?" she asked almost brightly.

"Didn't last night dampen your enthusiasm?" he asked. "I'd rather you stayed in London and kept watch over Shortwave."

"And I'd rather go with you," she said staunchly. "You promised. And anyway, we can leave Shortwave here with Mr Haroon."

"Aren't you awfully trusting?" the Saint said, pulling her into the kitchen to be certain that Haroon could not hear. "What if Abdul lets Shortwave go?"

"He wouldn't dare," she said. "For one thing. Shortwave would kill him for cooking up that curry."

"That's the sort of motive only a newspaper-woman could dream up," the Saint said. "Let me just say it straight out: I don't think you should come with me because it's too dangerous and because we don't need two people—especially one who's inclined to dive for the barrels of rifles when they're pointed right at her."

"I'm going," Tammy said.

"What about your car?" he suggested temptingly. "It's probably still lying wounded out in that ditch near Wraysbury. Shouldn't you take care of it?"

"I'll call up my paper and tell them what happened and they can see about the car."

"No, you won't," the Saint said firmly. "To Fowler and Kalki you're supposed to be dead, remember? You'll have to stay missing so that they don't change their plans for tonight. And, as I said, it would be a lot safer for you to stay missing right here."

"I won't stay here!" she persisted. "You promised me!"

Simon looked hard at her and shook his head with angry admiration.

"For that I should have my head examined," he said. "But if you're determined to have a hole in yours like Shortwave—"

As if the Saint's last word had been a stage cue, there was suddenly a horrendous uproar from the dining room.

Shortwave was yelling at the top of his voice: "Hey! Don't leave me! I just heard—they're gonna get me! D-d-d-don't leave me! I heard . . ."

3

"Just what did you hear?" Simon asked.

Shortwave, wild-eyed and sweating, scarcely managed to bring his vocal dam-burst under control. Abdul Haroon was as he had been when the Saint and Tammy had hurried in, speechless and staggered by the whole affair, sagging weakly against a wall.

"I heard they're gonna get me," Shortwave babbled. "It started working again, and I heard it."

"What started working again?" Tammy asked.

"My head," Shortwave said impatiently. "Like, you know, I can hear stuff, and just then I'm sittin' here and bang it starts up again and I hear a little bit of 'Tea for Two' and some static and then I hear Fowler saying to Kalki he better get me because I squealed . . ."

The little man ended his sentence not so much because he seemed to have run out of things to say as because his lungs ran out of air. While he was reinflating, Tammy rolled her eyes and tapped her temple with a forefinger for Simon's and Haroon's benefit. Simon nodded.

"I can't think why I should waste time soothing your psyche," he said to his captive, "but I can think of two reasons why you couldn't have heard that even if your circuits did warm up again. Number one, you're wired for radio transmissions, and I should think Kalki and Fowler would talk to one another on the telephone or in person. Number two, and much more significant they couldn't possibly know you squealed unless they'd been here five minutes ago . . . unless you're going to tell me they've got antennae of their own, and a network hook-up."

"I d-d-d-dunno, but I heard it. They know it, I'm telling you! It come through as clear as a bell. Wait a minute!" He stopped and listened intently staring at the table. *"The princess wore a trendy silk and organdie cocktail dress with matching . . ."* He looked up and shook his head with relief. "Naw, that ain't Fowler."

"Definitely not," agreed the Saint.

"But it was before!" Shortwave insisted.

"It was your guilty conscience," Tammy said sceptically. "It's high time you developed one."

"And leaving you with that edifying thought, we'll be on our way."

The most observant and objective judge would have had a hard time deciding whether it was Shortwave or Haroon who reacted more boisterously to that piece of news. They both began yawling at once, and out of the caterwauling came the general impression that neither of them wanted to be left anywhere—but above all else did they not want to be left there, especially not with one another.

"I cannot!" Haroon was wailing. "I cannot have it! I cannot, cannot, cannot!"

"You can't d-do this to me!" Shortwave yelped. "It's murder! They know I'm here—I heard it! You can't."

The Saint restored order by sheer force of personality. His firm calm voice, fortified by his commanding height and the unruffled authority of his stance, soon had the effect which oil is reputed to exercise on troubled waters.

"Neither one of you characters is in any position to argue," he said. "You'll do exactly as I say because you've got no choice." He looked down at Shortwave. "You're the little hero who wanted to slice up our gizzards last night, don't forget, and you're lucky the worst we're going to do to you for the moment is lock you up for the day." He turned to Haroon. "Where can we stow him?"

"You can't!" the owner cried. "There is no place!"

"What about his flat?" Tammy suggested.

"We can't get Shortwave up there without carrying him through the street," Simon told her, "Doesn't this place have a cellar, Abdul?"

"You cannot!"

Simon spoke like a man who sees the end of his patience in plain view just ahead.

"You'll do what I tell you or you'll be in jail before you know what hit you!"

Haroon yielded.

"Back here," he said. "The stairs are beyond the washroom."

Shortwave kept up a steady stream of protest while he was being transferred down to a small windowless basement which apparently served only as a sort of limbo for an assortment of junk that Haroon could find no use for but could not quite bring himself to throw out. There was a table with three legs, a chair with a broken back, a couple of cases of empty dust-caked wine bottles, a stack of cardboard cartons and boxes, and a rolled-up mattress with its stuffing protruding through multiple hernias.

"A lot cosier than a drum of wet cement," Simon said approvingly. "And if you're reasonably unobnoxious, maybe Mr Haroon will give you some more nice curry later in the day. You can put a gag on him before your hired hands come in for the evening, Abdul, and if he starts making a nuisance of himself pat him on the head with your biggest frying pan—and hope you don't bend the frying pan. I'm going to put in an anonymous tip to Scotland Yard to be on the lookout for him, just in case he figures some way to get loose . . . But if he does get loose, Abdul, I shall hold you responsible, and I mean totally responsible. If you don't want this admirable little eatery of yours to open under new management next week, while you settle down to lose a few pounds on good old British bread and water, you'll be absolutely sure that Shortwave is sitting right here when I come back. Is that clear?"

Haroon nodded vigorously. Having double-checked Shortwave's bonds and surroundings, the Saint came back up the steep stairs, closed the door at the top, and walked with Tammy and Haroon back to the rear of the restaurant.

"All right, Abdul, have a nice day, and good luck to you in finding some fresh staff. When Miss Rowan and I get finished you shouldn't have as many worries about keeping the personnel alive as you've had up till now. And you'll be able to breathe like a free man for the first time in—how long?"

Abdul Haroon grinned pallidly and used one of the English expressions on which he prided himself.

"In donkey's years," he said, and stood despondently waiting for the Saint and Tammy to drive away.

Tammy watched the pear-shaped restaurateur through the back window of the car until Simon had turned out of the alley into the street at the end.

"Do you think he'll be all right?" she asked.

"You could get better odds on his health than ours today, I think. If he does what I told him he shouldn't have any problems."

Tammy sat back in her seat and tried to relax.

"So we're headed for the sea?" she said.

"Right. After we've stopped by my place for breakfast, and your flat for a change of clothes."

"What'll we do when we get there? And I mean the sea—not your 'place,' wherever it is."

"Have a lovely time, of course. The sky is clear, the air is crisp. The only thing we don't know is how the water is. I should have asked Shortwave for the marine forecast."

Tammy smiled, stretched her arms, and clasped her hands behind her head.

"I think that wretched little beast is cracking up. I hope he spends the rest of his life thinking he's a television set with a burnt-out picture tube." She shivered involuntarily. "I'm so glad to be away from him, I just can't tell you! You know, I'm only just starting to realise how terrified I was last night."

4

But while Tammy was in the processing of cleansing Shortwave from her mind, Abdul Haroon was finding him considerably less easy to ignore.

The owner of the Golden Crescent had no sooner seen the Saint and his flaxen-haired passenger away from the back door and returned to his kitchen than the prisoner in the cellar began to shout and thump on the subterranean floor. The noise was well-muffled and could not have been heard in the street, but the ears of Abdul Haroon were made hypersensitive by anxiety. He had never been an optimistic man, and now it seemed to him that any revelation of his unwilling involvements with either Kalki or Simon Templar would lead to certain and total ruin.

He listened in anguish for a few minutes to Shortwave's uproar and then hurried out of the kitchen to the door at the top of the stairs. He rapped sharply on it.

"Stop it down there! Stop it!"

"Lemme out of here!" bawled Shortwave. "They're gonna kill me!"

Haroon opened the door, and his reply was in the style of a schoolmaster addressing an unruly pupil.

"You are very bad!" he said. "You must be quiet. You have heard what was said here, and I can do nothing."

The bumping below stopped. With his ear to the door, Haroon could hear the captive's heavy breathing, and then his moderated vicious voice, which unpleasantly resembled the hiss of a snake.

"Listen, you fat double-crosser, you let me out of here before they come to get me or I'll kill you!"

"You would try to kill me if I untied you," Haroon wisely replied. "You are crazy. Nobody is coming to get you because nobody knows you are here."

Shortwave's voice betrayed nerves that were as taut as banjo strings.

"They do know!" he exploded. "They know!" He paused for a second. "I know a few things too," he said in a new sly tone. "I've got enough on you to get you in twice as much trouble with the cops as Templar ever could. You hear me? If I do get out of here later I'll see they send you up for good—unless I get my hands on you first."

Haroon's knees felt weaker the more he reflected on the realism of Shortwave's threats. A little while before, as he was sincerely wishing the Saint well, he had felt that the burden which Kalki and Fowler had loaded on to his shoulders during the past months was at last really going to be lifted. Now all the hopelessness returned, and he began to see himself once more as a great soft brown rat trapped by cats in a maze.

"But if you help me I'll just let you alone and get out of here," Shortwave promised. "Come on, what's it to you?"

"The Saint would get me," Haroon mumbled.

"If he don't, Kalki will."

"No. Templar will take care of it all and come back." The words alone gave the fat man courage. "You just wait. You will see."

He left the cellar door and went back to the kitchen.

"Templar won't be back!" Shortwave screamed after him. "If you don't d-do something about me quick, it's gonna be too late, and Kalki's gonna get you!"

Haroon tried unsuccessfully to shut the words from his mind and turned to the one solace he had found in life of late: food. On the counter by the refrigerator he began assembling the ingredients for a culinary orgy whose very volume would be guaranteed to swamp his whole being and drive every worry from his heart.

But in the background Shortwave kept up his thumping and screaming at a more frenzied pitch than ever. Haroon's hands were shaking. He almost dropped a bowl of eggs. At some fancied sound behind him his heart stopped thudding for a full two seconds. He sank his unsteady fingers into a cold baked chicken, tore it in half, and imagined the similar fate that awaited him if Kalki or Fowler should find that he was keeping one of their group a prisoner—and that he had collaborated in other ways to help their enemies.

Shortwave's screeching suddenly became unbearable. Haroon snatched up just such a large iron frying pan as the Saint had suggested to him for maintaining peace in his own house and ran heavily back to the cellar door. He started down the stairs, clutching the banister, with the big skillet raised on high in his free hand. The instant Shortwave saw it he cringed and grew as quiet as a laryngitic giraffe. Haroon brandished the pan.

"Be quiet or I will kill you myself," he threatened hoarsely.

Shortwave, still bound hand and foot, could only cower and attempt to wring out every last drop of his meagre dramatic ability in what he considered a final attempt to save himself. He had genuinely thought he had tuned in on Kalki and Fowler's plans to kill him for betraying them. There were other moments when his cacophonous mentality reminded him of the logic of the Saint's argument that

Fowler could not possibly know what had happened over the curry bowl in the dining room of the Golden Crescent. The facts and fantasies were so jumbled in his steel-reinforced head by now that they rang like loose bolts in a metal bucket.

"Would you let this guy Templar cut my throat?" he asked Haroon almost tearfully.

"No!" said Haroon, and meant it.

Shortwave knew he meant it. In his nightmare imagination he saw Kalki flexing his giant hands and coming after him. The only hope was to make amends.

"Look, Abdul," Shortwave argued, "if they show up here we've both had it. We gotta let them know I didn't mean it. Now go call up Kalki in case he d-d-didn't leave yet and tell him the Saint got loose last night and he's on his way after Fowler and I said to warn them. You got that? We get off the hook that way, see? See how easy it is? Come on, Abdul—do me a favour and just call him, right now. Okay?"

Haroon had lowered the frying pan and was listening. The multiplying changes of pace, from menace to supplication, were starting to unhinge the precarious stability of whatever powers of discrimination he might once have possessed.

"Why should I call, you fool? They know nothing now."

Shortwave decided to humour him.

"Okay, Abdul, so they don't know. All the more reason to call. Let 'em know how we're both trying to help out. Just don't tell Kalki anything, okay? I mean about what either one of us done. Just tell him I said to tell him the Saint knows."

Abdul Haroon was tempted. His fear of the police was becoming distinctly remote from his reburgeoning fear of Kalki. But he said nothing. He was considering.

Shortwave got panicky again at the possibility of refusal.

"You got to," he begged. "Think what they'll do to us. Remember Ali? I mean, man, it won't be nice! I'd rather do anything—I'd rather go to jail than let Kalki get his hands on me. What can the Saint do? Nothing! He's just bluffing you. Let me loose, okay?"

"No."

But Haroon was quivering. His chubby legs had all the sturdiness of wet rice paper.

"Then if you won't let me loose call up Kalki, but quick! Tell him before it's too late!"

The fat man's resolution wilted. He began nodding assent, did not bother to close the cellar door, and trotted away across the dining room, and out on to the pavement. He was running for the telephone in his flat, one of his hands fluttering like a bird and the other still clutching his frying pan. He did not even realise that he was carrying the pan until he started feverishly to dial Kalki's number.

A moment later the voice of the wrestler answered.

"Good, good!" Abdul Haroon began. "I was afraid you might have gone. This is Haroon. I . . . I must tell you that the Saint knows about you and Fowler."

"The Saint is dead," Kalki said tolerantly.

"No, he is not!" Haroon blurted. "He was here just half an hour ago! With Shortwave!"

Kalki roared like a typhoon. Interspersed in the general detonation were appropriate questions. Haroon melted onto his sofa like warm jelly, fairly blubbering into the mouthpiece.

"It was not my fault! Shortwave told them where Fowler would be tonight. They left him here tied up. I could do nothing but hurry to ring you. You see, I have warned you! I have done all I could!"

"And where is the Saint?"

"On his way to the fort."

"And Shortwave?"

"Still here, still tied."

"I will be there in five minutes! Open the door for me!"

The line clicked dead at Kalki's end.

Haroon hauled himself to his feet, muttered incoherently to himself, turned around three times, started off in one direction and then in another, and finally ran to the chest of drawers in his bedroom. He took out his wallet, stuffed it with what cash he had hidden in the flat, looped a tie around his bulging neck, jerked a knot into it, grabbed up a jacket and topcoat, and set off down the stairs. Halfway down he remembered some negotiable cheques, heaved his bulk up the steps again, retrieved them, and waddled down again.

Kalki lived so close by that he might easily have been in front of the restaurant already. Haroon opened the door and started to step into the dining room, but then considered the possibilities of entrapment if Kalki should arrive and come in after him.

"D-d-did you call?" Shortwave shouted anxiously from the depths of the basement. "Did you get him?"

"Yes!" Haroon answered shrilly.

Then he wondered why he had answered. He wondered why he was there at all. He could have been running. But he was afraid that by running he might anger Kalki even more. Instead he left the door slightly ajar, and stood outside it in the brightening sunlight, revelling in the safety of the public pavement, where taxies and lorries flew this way and that, and people were everywhere.

He was all but dancing on his toes in front of his place of business when Kalki the Conqueror loomed into view around the corner, his whiskers swept by the breeze of his striding speed. He wore a red waistcoat and a plaid jacket, and his black ball-bearing eyes were so close together as to seem fused and inseparable.

Haroon kept himself at least ten feet away, backing off as Kalki approached.

Kalki did not say anything but: "Where?"

Haroon pointed to the open door. The passers-by hurried around him in the sunshine, seeing nothing strange. Only when Kalki had stalked into the restaurant did Haroon venture nearer. Still standing well back from the threshold he peered inside and ascertained that Kalki had gone on towards the rear of the premises. Then he edged into the doorway, leaving most of his mass outside in the sun while he extended his neck in order to hear what was happening.

The strange thing was that he heard nothing. He had expected screams and roars. He had to sidle halfway across the dining room before he detected the sounds of voices. Before he could make out the words the voices abruptly stopped. The silence was then stranger than ever. Straining his senses, Haroon heard a sound like a gasp of air escaping briefly from a balloon, and then a noise like the crushing of an eggshell.

Abdul Haroon turned and fled, his coattails flapping, and did not stop running until he was in a taxi bound for Victoria Station and the next train from London to anywhere else.

CHAPTER SIX:

HOW KALKI TOOK A DIVE AND SIMON TEMPLAR MADE HIS PROFIT

1

Highway A13 out of London follows the northside curves of the widening Thames where the river opens its mouth to the North Sea. The Dartford Tunnel, on the eastern rim of the city, is the last man-made spanning of the estuary. From there on the water is free of all traffic except boats, fish, and seagulls, though its banks are burdened with the giant chimneys of power stations and the cranes of dockyards—skeletal forests like burnt-out woodlands with the smokey haze of their extinction still hanging over them.

Even though the river soon becomes so broad that it would be better called a gulf, and half an hour farther east expands so far as to become indistinguishable from the sea, the smokestacks of the power stations remained a constant landmark down to the Saint's right as he drove along the highway. At first they dominated the landscape entirely. They were supplanted by their monstrous stepsons, great towers of steel which carried the high tension power lines across the countryside on their shoulders.

But even those ventured only as occasional stragglers very far from the complex that spawned them. Huge lorries rolled on across Essex, but the countryside gradually turned less commercial. Oil storage tanks looked lost in open fields amongst signs offering "New Laid Eggs" and "Home Grown Potatoes." There was a Donkey Derby at One Tree Hill, and a more hopeful signal in the form of a beat-up old boat in somebody's front garden.

"How far do we have to go before we take to the water?" Tammy asked the Saint.

She sounded admirably calm, but he noticed that her fingers kept fiddling with the leather strap of the binoculars he had brought from his house in Upper Berkeley Mews before they left London.

"No farther than we have to," he said. "But we've all day, and we might as well enjoy it. How are we looking on the chart?"

"There's a picture of a sailboat at South Benfleet," she told him, tracing their route on a map of southeast England. It's not far off this road."

"That's probably where Fowler's boat stops over on these runs," Simon remarked. "But I don't think he'll be there himself as early as this. Keep your fingers crossed, though."

"Turn right at Great Tarpots," said Tammy.

They negotiated a roundabout south of Basildon and drove through an area heavily built up with houses. But down on the right they could see the marshy banks of the last official few miles of the Thames. The water even then no longer looked like a river: it was a broad expanse glaring in the light of the low sun.

The Saint slowed down. Great Tarpots might once have been conspicuous enough to merit its grandiose name, but now it appeared to have been lost in the general spread of dwellings and shops between Basildon and Thundersley. The turn to South Benfleet was marked not only by an appropriate road sign, but also by the more ominous presence on the corner of "Alden & Sons, Funerals and Memorials."

"That's promising," Tammy observed.

"Maybe we should make advance reservations for Fowler and Kalki," was the Saint's more optimistic reply. "But on second thoughts it'd be cheaper to give the fish a treat."

It was the time of the mid-morning break now, and the residential streets were full of schoolgirls in uniform skirts and jackets and boy-style neckties. But within a mile or so the unwelcome dampness of the river's tidal banks kept homes at a distance. The fenced premises of the Benfleet Yacht Club were an encouraging sight, even though its vessels were for members only.

Simon slowed down. Just ahead was a swing bridge, and the creek it crossed was lined with half-floating sail- and motor-boats. The tide was fairly low. Simon could only hope that it was coming in rather than going out. Otherwise the creek looked barely navigable.

He managed to find a place to park his car just off the road, and he and Tammy walked to the nearest of several establishments along the creek which dealt in boats. It was a barren place, with grassy mud flats crisscrossed with shallow reeking ditches where shellfish must have spent at least half their lives dying at low tide. The wooden building looked no friendlier, and neither did the boaty type who stepped out with a one-eyed mongrel dog at his side to meet the Saint and his companion.

"I'd like to hire a sailboat," Simon told him after a cautious exchange of greetings.

The Saint stood with his hands in his pockets while the other man mulled over the question.

"It's not easy to hire a boat around here."

"There seem to be plenty of them," Simon rejoined.

As the man answered, it seemed that he was more reserved than unfriendly.

"You'd be better off around at Thorpe Bay or someplace like that," he said. "We've had bad luck hiring boats to people in these tidal waters. The creek'll be two foot deep in one spot and twenty foot deep in another, and when the tide goes out they'll run aground and walk off and leave the boat, and then the tide comes in and the boat turns up floating on the Canvey front and we've got to go and fetch it."

At least he had not said no.

"You don't have to worry," Simon said. "I won't run aground and I won't abandon your boat."

"How long do you want it for?"

"A few hours—most of the day, probably."

The boatman looked out across the mud and water. The sky was clear and bright, with only a few small clouds above the distant smoke-stacks and their windblown plumes of white steam.

"Should be a nice day." He sampled the crustacean-scented atmosphere with his nose. "But it's not very warm. Not much of a time for being out on the water."

"We're hardy types," the Saint assured him. "We belong to the Polar Bear Club. We take a dip in the sea every Christmas Day."

The man facing him huddled down inside several layers of sweaters and a duffle coat.

"You're welcome to it," he said. "But you'd be better off around at Thorpe Bay or someplace."

"How much does it cost to hire a boat when you do hire one?" Simon interrupted.

The man paused to ponder how much he might get.

"Two pounds an hour for a boat big enough to be even halfway safe out there this time of year." He shook his head. "But I just don't want to take a chance. I'm sorry."

Simon had already spotted a likely looking if weather-beaten craft in the water near the wooden building.

"How much would that cost?" he asked.

"I told you—"

"I mean how much would it cost if I just took it out and sank it—which I don't intend to do, incidentally."

"It's not for sale, but if it was I reckon it might bring two hundred quid."

Simon did not bat an eye at the vast overestimate. He reached inside the weatherproof tan jacket he was wearing and pulled out a wallet. From the wallet he counted fifteen ten-pound notes.

"Deposit," he said, offering them to the other man, who had been watching with rapidly expanding interest. "That should make it worth your while even if you had to go down to Canvey to fetch it—which you won't."

The man looked at the money and then at the Saint.

"You really mean it?"

"Take it," Simon said.

The man took it, took his customers into the building, and laboriously wrote out a receipt. Then he started getting the boat rigged with sails, all the while giving directions for negotiating the creek which would have appalled a Mississippi riverboat captain.

"You're lucky the tide's coming in," he said. "Makes it a little easier."

"I'll go fetch our lunch," Simon said.

He set off back to the car for the picnic provisions which he had thoughtfully packed in Upper Berkeley Mews—some cold tongue and ham, bread and butter, apples, cans of beer in a thermal bag full of ice cubes, and a flask of martinis. Tammy followed him.

"Don't you think we should get one with a motor on it?" she muttered. "I mean, we've got a pistol and binoculars and a flashlight, but not water wings. I'd hate to have to swim back."

"We've got to look innocent," Simon said. "In a sailboat, we can drift about and tack around the fort in all directions, without looking as if it was our special target. But at the first sign that we're not a couple of lovebirds enjoying a sail, we'll become a couple of sitting ducks in a shooting gallery."

The boat owner was busy with the sails when they returned with their burdens. Tammy gazed pessimistically at the boat, which bore the name *Sunny Hours*. It appeared to have seen many a sunny hour, and many a stormy one as well. Possibly it would look bright and new after its winter renovation, but right now it looked fit for piecemeal consumption on a fireplace.

It floated, however. Simon took the tiller, Tammy got herself more or less comfortably installed beside him, and the owner waded out in boots to get the craft into deeper water.

"Well," said Simon as the southerly breeze caught the sails, "wish us bon voyage."

"Good luck," the boatman said dubiously.

It was a long awkward run that they made down the variable waters of the creek, but the channel widened after a while, and at last the *Sunny Hours* spread her wings in the open river. She had no company except wheeling gulls and a long barge churning its way slowly in the opposite direction towards London.

"I don't see any forts," Tammy said, peering ahead.

"They're out there somewhere," Simon assured her. "We're still in the river until we get abeam of Southend. Just enjoy yourself. We've got a long way to go yet."

"And when the sun sinks in the west, so do we?"

Simon smiled at her.

"Think positively. It's Fowler who's going to get sunk. Relax."

The dead forest of smokestacks lay small in the haze behind them. The mouth of the creek from which they had entered the Thames was lost in the dwindling line of the shore. There was no need for tacking. The wind was almost on the starboard beam, growing fresher. The pressure of the sail strained hard against Simon's hand and as the boat's speed increased the water gurgled and coiled away from the rudder in a thin white wake. There was a perceptible rolling when they encountered bigger waves farther from the shore.

"Cor," Tammy said. "I wish the wind would let up a bit."

"Don't say things like that," the Saint warned her. "We seafaring men are notoriously superstitious. All we need to scuttle the whole operation is to get ourselves becalmed."

"Fat chance of that," Tammy said, clinging to the side of the boat as it swung skittishly from a swell to a trough.

"Speaking of fat, I wonder how Abdul's getting along," Simon said.

"What can go wrong?" Tammy asked.

"Abdul can," the Saint replied. "He's got the moral fibre of a three-week-old stick of celery."

"Well, there's no point worrying about that. We've not only crossed the Rubicon—we're right in the middle of it." She stopped suddenly and pointed towards the horizon. "What's that over there?"

Simon pulled a maritime chart out of one of the large pockets of his windbreaker and with Tammy's help spread it on his knees.

"It is one of the forts," he said after a moment. "But it's the wrong one. Too close in. The one we want has to be somewhere off Shoeburyness. That would be at least thirteen miles from where we started."

"How lucky," Tammy commented.

Simon adjusted his course slightly. They were far from the nearest land now. To the north, the Essex coastline was almost parallel to their course. Kent, to the south, curved sharply away into the distance, but was mostly lost in a yellowish mist that seemed absent over the water itself. The fort they had seen was scarcely more than a darkish silvery point, and they drew no closer to it.

For a long time they sailed on. After a while it was like being on the open sea, but their rate of travel was becoming slower. The sheet was tugging less forcefully against Simon's hand. He tensely endured the slackening of the wind for almost half an hour before saying anything.

"You've done it," he said to Tammy at last.

"Done what?"

"Wished us into trouble. The wind is dropping. We are about to become the victims of light airs."

"What are they?" she asked anxiously.

"They are airs of insufficient velocity to move a boat with any rapidity through the water. In short, if things get much worse we could be sitting here watching on some very wet sidelines while Fowler does what he pleases."

Tammy put one of her hands into the water and watched the surface break around it.

"We're still moving," she said.

"About half as fast as we were before you jinxed the wind," he retorted.

The sail became slacker. It had carried them less than half the distance to the island when Tammy tested the relative motion of the water again. There wasn't any.

"We've stopped," she said meekly.

The sail hung from the mast with dejected limpness. The erstwhile waves had become oily swells.

"I told you we should have had something with an engine," she said.

"We've got something better: we've got martinis," said the Saint cheerfully. "Since we can't anchor out here, this seems a good time to have lunch. There must be a certain amount of current from the flow of the river, so we still ought to be drifting in the right direction. Fowler isn't supposed to make his pick-up till late in the afternoon, and this calm won't last forever unless you do some more reckless wishing."

Without the wind, the sun was warm enough for the Saint to enjoy taking off his shirt, and for Tammy to peel off her jeans and sit in the short shorts which she had providently worn underneath. The martinis, lunch, and cold beer made a happy interlude that was only incongruous when either of them had a recollection of the mission that had brought them out there, of what had preceded it, and what grim climax could be waiting at the end of the day. But Simon Templar could enjoy any pleasurable intermission for itself alone, and for him there was unalloyed pleasure in contemplating the sunlight on Tammy's shapely legs, and the spontaneous expressions that chased over her impish face.

They were far enough north of the main navigation channels to be untroubled by the regular passage of lighters, freighters, tankers, and an occasional passenger steamship bound in and out of the Port of London. A few small sailboats, to the north, attempted to offer canvas to the unseasonable lull, but most of their potential masters and crew seemed to be less hardy souls who were already trending towards their regular autumnal retreat. A speedboat of two creamed ostentatiously over the inshore mud flats . . . And after many long lulls, Tammy suddenly cried "Look!"

She was gesturing towards a new silvery point in the water. Simon had missed seeing it before because he had not been urgently looking for it, and in any case the sail had been in his way. He let his craft come about into the weakly reviving wind while he focused his binoculars on the object. It was near the eastern horizon, and he half expected it to be another boat. But a combination of tide and current must have carried them farther than he would have estimated. What he was looking at was distinctly not a boat, even though it bobbed so much in his field of view because of his own motion that he could not make out any details.

"That must be it," he said after consulting his chart again. "Now all we have to do is get there."

He looked at the position of the sun as he got the boat under control again. There would still be plenty more daylight. It now seemed possible—if the wind did not give out again—that he could reach the fort before Fowler did, or at least before he left with his cargo. Assuming that Shortwave was right when he said that Fowler would not make his coastal landing before dark. But there were still plenty of dicey unknowns in the equation: one was that Fowler might already be there, and the other was that he might arrive by fast boat while the *Sunny Hours* was manoeuvring for a landing.

"Do you know how to sail?" Simon asked Tammy.

"I can do anything," Tammy said. "Why? Are you tired?"

"No, but I was thinking that no matter when we get to Fowler's halfway house you're going to have to take over. If I'd come alone I'd just have set the boat adrift when I got to the fort and either tracked it down later or lost my hundred and fifty pounds. But now you can take it over when we get there and then move off to a safe distance while I become a one-man boarding party."

"I don't think I like that idea very much."

"Would you rather assume Fowler is so shortsighted that he won't see a sailboat tied up to his own hideout?"

"I'd rather come with you."

"We'll see when we get there," he said. "Meanwhile, you may be the greatest female sailor in the world, but it probably wouldn't hurt you to freshen up your technique."

He handed over the tiller and sheet, and it was only after she had turned the boat completely around twice without making head way in any direction that he intervened.

"I thought you said you could do anything," he said blandly. "It's a good thing there isn't much wind or you'd have swamped us."

"I meant I could learn to do anything," she said. "I didn't say I knew how already."

"We'd better have some lessons then. Just try to stay directly between the sun and the fort. In case somebody's out there with binoculars or a telescope the glare will keep him from making out too many details."

The slowly rising breeze was fitful but still powerful enough to fill the sails, and for an hour Tammy learned the rudiments of handling a small boat on a very big body of water. Her studies were cut shorter than they might have been when the Saint caught a glimpse of something out of the corner of his eye which was not the slowly growing fort on the horizon. He turned quickly and saw that it was a small speedboat racing towards them from the west. Without wasting time to explain, he took the tiller and sail away from Tammy and turned the bow of the *Sunny Hours* away from the fort, and also away from the approaching speedboat.

"What have I done now?" she demanded angrily. "I was just getting the idea."

"You see that boat? Take a look at it through the binoculars and tell me all about it."

"You don't think it's somebody after us?" she asked in alarm.

"There's no harm in finding out before they get here," Simon replied. "Take a look."

The boat was a mile or more away, and Tammy had to look for some time, adjusting the focus, before she felt certain enough of anything to start giving a report.

"It's not a very big boat but it's moving fast," she said. "It's open. No roof. I think there's . . . one man. Just one." She brought the eyepieces of the binoculars away from her eyes and looked at the Saint. "Do you think it's Fowler?"

"You tell me. I'm busy making like an agonised amateur trying to sail around the world backwards."

The girl squinted through the glasses again.

"Oh, no," she breathed.

"Fowler?"

"No. I can't really make out his face, but I've got a strong feeling . . . I'm sure it is: Kalki!"

"Ah, the Flying Hindu," Simon said. "And he's alone?"

At the same time, he was quietly taking his automatic out of an inner pocket of his discarded windbreaker, and double-checking its load and readiness for action.

"There's nobody with him," Tammy said. "That's something anyway. Perhaps Fowler's already on the fort—or coming out later."

"Isn't he headed for us?" Simon asked, turning to look for himself.

"No. I don't think so. He's curving around in the direction of the fort."

"That's good news." He tucked his gun back under the folded jacket. "But now we can't risk getting too near the fort in full daylight. I'll make a long sweep around and come up on it towards sunset from the southwest, when the sun will be right in their eyes." He was talking as much to himself as to Tammy. "I seem to have thought of everything except bringing a couple of false beards for us to disguise ourselves if anyone starts watching us with a good pair of glasses."

"May I practise some more?" Tammy asked.

He offered her the tiller.

"Be my guest. Keep the fort well to your left, and try to keep your face turned away from it. Not that it isn't a pretty face, but why give the Ungodly a treat they don't deserve?"

"Aye-aye, Commodore."

"I'll stand watch . . . from here."

And with that the Saint stretched out on the bottom of the boat with his head on a lifejacket, and to all appearances fell promptly fast asleep.

2

The insignificant white form of a sailboat off his starboard side did not even remotely influence the rush of Kalki's thoughts as he bore down on the fort. Fowler would be infuriated to see him racing out in broad daylight, but there was no choice. When the giant wrestler had learned that the Saint was free and on his trail—undoubtedly, Kalki's inaccurate imagination told him, with a sizeable entourage of newspaper reporters and policemen—his first impulse after venting his rage in the execution of Shortwave was to run for his life.

One thing in particular stopped him: the cash which he and Fowler had stored at the fort. It amounted to the proceeds from the last several shipments of immigrants. As long as things had been going smoothly there had been no need for either him or Fowler to distrust the other; it was too profitable to both of them to continue their partnership. But now that crisis was upon them, the cash, in several national currencies, suddenly became very important. Kalki liked fine clothes and expensive Soho ladies. He was not a thrifty man. If he was to fly away to some haven across the sea, perhaps in the West Indies, he would need his share of that money. He would also have to be sure that no evidence—say in the form of a dozen talkative Indians and Pakistanis—was left wandering about the littoral to further threaten his future.

He was not particularly worried about Fowler's running away with all the money for a very simple reason: both men, by mutual understanding, had deposited with their separate lawyers in sealed envelopes small but damning sheets of paper on which incriminating facts about the opposite partner were detailed. Each lawyer had instructions to open the envelope in his possession in the event of the death of his client through other than unmistakable natural causes. While full of hazards, the arrangement had given some stability to an otherwise even more touchy situation.

But like all such arrangements it had its limitations, and Kalki saw this as the get-out point.

When he piloted his outboard up to the fort there was no trace of life on the big platform. The deck of the structure rested on six huge round supports which were sunk into the sea bottom. Even at high tide the water level did not ever approach the platform, and at this stage of rising tide a foot or so of barnacles still showed on the round legs. The shelters on top of the platform looked as disused as they were supposed to be. Their metal walls were etched with red rust where the greyish silver paint had chipped away.

Kalki cut the boat's engine and drifted up against one of the steel legs of the fort. A series of ladder steps, towel-rack style, were welded on to the leg. He made the bow line of his boat fast to one of the rungs, let the boat swing round under the shadow of the platform, and then hauled his great bulk up the ladder to the platform.

Fowler stepped from beside the wall of a metal shed.

"What the hell are you doing here?" he growled.

"The Saint is loose," Kalki said without preface. "Shortwave told him you were coming out here."

The two of them stood back against the wall while Fowler delivered himself to some choicely worded opinions of Shortwave, the Saint, and the nature of the universe in general. Kalki filled him in on such parts of the story as he could.

Fowler grated his bottom teeth against the top ones and looked at the lowering sun.

"I don't know," he said tensely. "If it was dark . . . or we had a fog . . . What the devil am I going to do with that cargo in there? I can't run them to shore now."

Kalki had already pondered that problem.

"We got to get rid of them," he said.

Fowler snorted.

"You're the magician, then. Go right ahead and make the whole lot disappear in a puff of smoke."

"Put them in your boat and take them out and sink it," Kalki said. "It is too dangerous to take them ashore or to leave them here. Nobody will ever know what happened if you sink them in the sea."

Fowler's mind, which had long ago adjusted itself to an essential killing here and there, as long as somebody else did it and he was not around, was so unprepared for the thought of mass murder that he automatically began to protest.

"You listen to me!" Kalki interrupted, bringing his face down close in front of Fowler's. "You can stay here and be a nanny to them if you want to, but I want my half of the money and I want to get out of here before the Saint shows up."

Fowler glanced towards the sun again. There was a bank of haze and clouds coming to meet it from the west, turning the sky a deep yellow-red.

"All right," he said in total desperation. "It'll have to be done that way. Go watch for anything coming this way while I get the men in my boat."

"Now?" Kalki asked, following Fowler's eyes towards the sun.

"Now. I'll lock them below and tell them we'll go ashore as soon as it's dark."

"But you will take them out now?"

"Not unless we see trouble coming. I'd still rather wait until after dark. Keep an eye open for any fast boats coming this way. As soon as it's dark I'll run them out while you follow in the outboard. You pick me up as soon as I've made a good-sized hole in the hull."

Kalki followed him towards the door of the shed.

"You'd better watch out for boats," Fowler told him again.

"I want my half of the money."

"And to leave me stuck in a sinking ship? I'll take it all out with me. You'll be right behind. We'll divvy it up when we've got this job finished."

Fowler's hand was in his blazer pocket, and Kalki knew that Fowler would not let the price of some invisible mending keep him from firing through the fabric and putting a very visible hole in Kalki.

"All right," the Pakistani said. "I'll stay out here."

"And I'll go tell these twelve poor buggers they're bound for the Promised Land . . ."

3

"Simon . . ." Tammy said. "Simon?"

The Saint lifted his head from his makeshift pillow and looked at her. He had never been in a deep sleep. He had been continuously aware of the gradations of changing light which had now left the sky grey with the dusk.

"How are we doing?"

"I think the breeze is getting stronger."

"It's probably just the backwash from a passing seagull."

"No, seriously, it is."

He sat up and moved to take over control of the sailboat. The fort was only a few hundred yards away, marked with dim red warning lights.

"I don't see how you can relax at a time like this," Tammy said petulantly. "What if they'd got away?"

"You'd have told me. But our relaxing hours are over now. I'm heading straight in to the stronghold of the evildoers. I'm just surprised no other boat has come out there."

"Why?"

"Well, I assumed that Fowler must already be there. Otherwise why would Kalki be dashing out in the middle of the afternoon just to sit around and wait until nightfall." As the Saint was speaking he was setting the *Sunny Hours* on a direct course for the fort. He would bear to the north of it and come in against the wind. "But if Fowler's out there, why isn't there a bigger boat? That pea pod that Kalki went out in isn't big enough to carry the owl and the pussy cat in addition to Kalki and Fowler—much less a mixed bag of assorted grown men."

"Perhaps somebody else brings the boat out after dark."

"Possibly. But why would Fowler bother to go out—assuming somebody gave him a lift to the fort and left him—without his boat? It sounds very inefficient." The Saint had often found that the way to find answers was to think the unthinkable. The technique worked now. "Unless the boat is there."

"Wouldn't we have seen it through the binoculars? And wouldn't it be too dangerous for him to risk somebody seeing it? A lot of boats pass here during the day."

"We'll see when we get there," Simon said. "Which won't be long now."

The sailboat cut quietly through the smooth swell. The wind was freshening, but still not enough to raise a chop on the surface of the estuary. The Saint did not say so, but he was worried now—worried that he might be too late. If Fowler had a boat concealed at the fort there was nothing to stop him from leaving almost immediately.

The dark shape of the metal monster that was their goal loomed against the sky only a hundred yards away. Suddenly Simon pushed the tiller hard alee.

"Get down," he snapped at Tammy.

The swinging boom missed her head, but just barely.

"What's the matter?' she asked angrily.

"I think I saw something move along the rail up there. They'll be watching. I can't risk taking this boat right up under their noses. I'm going to sail past the fort, and roll over the side as we go by. Don't worry when you don't see me come up—I'll be swimming under water."

He leaned forward, wanting somehow to push the boat along faster by sheer force of will. Precious moments were ticking by with each gurgle of water that passed the *Sunny Hours'* prow.

"Wrap this pistol in that plastic bag for me, would you?" he said. "And here's what you do when I'm over the side: it'll take me a few minutes to swim to the fort."

"How'll you get on it? It's standing up on those high stilts."

"There must be a way. When you figure I'm getting near it, make some noise. Bang something on the bottom of the boat, as if you'd dropped it. And turn on the flashlight. Don't let the light get on your face or reflect on it. Just aim it up at the top of the sail as if you think something's gone wrong there. You should be a goodish way from the fort by that time, so they can't possibly recognise you or think you're somebody after them. But with someone around they'll wait a bit before leaving. I'd try distracting them now, but I don't want them to get too interested too soon."

It took only a few more minutes for Simon to get his small boat into position. The last glow of the sunset had disappeared, but he had a feeling that even in the darkening twilight the eyes which watched from the fort might have detected the dirty white sail against the dark water.

He let go the tiller, and the boat came up into the wind, the sail starting to flutter.

"Okay," he said quietly. "This is it. As soon as I've gone, head in towards those lights on the shore. In about three minutes stop just the way I've done and perform your little act with the flashlight. Then put out the light and keep going towards the coast. Let them know then that you're not interested in the fort."

"What about you?"

"I'll be busy. Stay off at a safe distance—especially if you hear a boat starting up. I'll give you a shout, or come and find you. Stay out between those lights and the fort so I know the general area you're in."

"What if . . ."

"What if what?"

"What if you don't shout or come and find me?"

He pointed north in the direction of the Essex shoreline.

"There's a lot of England thataway. You couldn't miss it if you tried. And when you run aground, it'll only be a muddy but easy walk to dry land."

"Good luck," she said, touching his hand.

"Thanks." He zipped the pistol into his jacket, lying full length along the gunwale. "Man overboard."

Then he rolled off horizontally into the icy water and struck out for the fort without surfacing. After covering a sufficient distance, he let his head come up just long enough to take a breath, to see that Tammy was under way again, and to relocate the fort. Then he slid back under the low swells like a seal and swam submerged with all the power he could command until his lungs were close to their limit of endurance.

When he came up again, he found that he was actually under the fort, having passed between two of the pilings it stood on without touching them. He was looking up from almost directly under the edge of the platform, which was fifteen feet or so above his head: only about thirty feet away from where Kalki's boat was tied to the bottom ladder rung on one of the great cylindrical supports of the structure.

Then he heard a clattering noise behind him, and pulled his way into hiding around the nearest column and looked back. A light danced on the sail on the *Sunny Hours* some two hundred yards away.

Above, he could hear footsteps on the metal deck of the platform.

"Wait a minute!" a muffled voice called. "There's that boat out there."

The voice, he was certain, was Kalki's. There were other hurried foot thumps on another part of the deck. He could not make out the words of the interchange that followed, but there was some very excited consultation going on. Simon took advantage of the distraction to swim swiftly but silently over to the leg of the fort where Kalki's motorboat was moored. There was, he decided, no need to climb up onto the platform of the fort itself: he could wait there and make his move when the other men came down. On the ladder rungs, with their backs to him, they would be at the disadvantage.

"I think it's going away."

"Can you see?"

"It's going away. They couldn't be looking for us. It's some fool who doesn't know how to sail."

Kalki and Fowler were speaking in voices of normal volume now that they no longer feared an immediate attack. The Saint looked over Kalki's boat as he listened to the conversation.

"You have an axe on board?" Kalki was asking.

"Yes," Fowler answered. "Don't worry about the way I do my part. And I've got a rubber raft and flares. If you ran out on me I might not spend a comfortable night, but I'd survive—and in that case I can promise you I'd survive a lot longer than you will."

"Do you threaten me," Kalki replied in a haughty voice.

"Just be sure you get up alongside before I sink."

"Don't worry," Kalki said. "The money would sink with you."

Fowler's rejoinder might have been edifying, but the Saint was now more interested in a little scheme he had conceived, involving the rope and heavy anchor which were perched on the bow of Kalki's boat. He busied himself cutting the rope loose while the men above him made their last-minute preparations for leaving.

A moment later he heard a new sound above him. He lowered himself back into the cold water, clinging to the side of the speedboat. A very large sliding panel in the bottom of the platform was sliding back, and a dim shielded light showed him just enough to explain Fowler's means of getting to and from the fort, and why it had not been visible from the *Sunny Hours*.

Above the opening in the bottom of the platform swung a cabin cruiser in a cradle. It could have been that the whole installation had been built into the original fort. Or it could have been that Fowler had managed to rig it up himself. In any case, the boat was there, and to the creak of pulleys and the metallic grinding of a winch it began to sink down through the opening and descend towards the surface of the water.

The Saint quickly dived under the hull of Kalki's smaller boat and re-emerged on the far side, keeping his head well down in the water. He heard the cradle and keel of Fowler's boat settle into the sloshing swells of the estuary, and the winch overhead ground to a stop.

"Right!" Fowler's voice called from just a few feet away. "I'll get going. Follow my lights as soon as you can—but lock up first. We might want to use this place again when Templar's out of the way."

Simon heard the platform's sliding panel groaning back into place, and over it the engine of Fowler's cruiser, as it spat and coughed and grumbled into full life. He heard it pull away slowly, scraping lightly against one of the far legs of the fort, before it began to pick up speed.

Up above, Kalki was wasting no time. Simon heard him slam a metal door, rattle something, and then run across the metal deck. A moment later his large feet appeared on the topmost rung of the ladder.

The Saint was waiting in the water when Kalki reached the bottom of the ladder and stretched out a leg to grope for the side of his boat.

Simon's actions were lightning-swift and simple: he had formed the end of the anchor rope into a noose.

He slipped the loop around Kalki's ankle, jerked it tight, and swung several half-hitches around the giant's leg.

Kalki was taken so completely by surprise that he could only bellow, kick, and try to climb back up the ladder. Which only pulled the knots tighter.

"Give up?" Simon asked. "If you're a good boy I'll just tie you up and leave you for the cops."

In time he saw Kalki's fist stretch out from his body, clutching a small revolver. The Saint's next act was even more deadly in its simplicity than the looping of the rope: he grasped the anchor and pulled it out over the side into the water. At the same moment as its weight came on the rope, he added his own weight to it.

The sudden shock of the combination jerked Kalki's hand and foot clean away from the ladder. With a howl he sailed over Simon's head, and the splash of the anchor was followed by the splash of Kalki. The howl was instantly swallowed up too, and there was only the sound of the water washing against the piers of the fort.

Simon hoisted himself with lithe agility into the speedboat and waited for a minute or two with his automatic in hand to see if Kalki's great strength would be enough to overcome about fifteen kilos of iron ballast. The seconds passed. Simon quietly put the gun back into the pocket of his dripping trousers. Kalki would break no more bones.

The Saint found a black slicker and hat in the boat. He put them on, started the motor, and cast off in pursuit of Fowler.

It was not a long chase. The lights of Fowler's cruiser came into sight far ahead of him in the open water. It was simple then to follow, but it was important not to come too close. If Fowler should turn a spotlight on him and recognise that it was not his partner, Kalki, in the following boat, things would become considerably more complicated.

He would have to time his approach carefully, coming up to Fowler when Fowler's attention was diverted.

They churned on out to sea, Simon's boat two hundred yards behind Fowler's. Finally the Saint found the distance between himself and the bigger craft narrowing. The cruiser had stopped. He cut his own power, holding back. Over the splashing waves he heard a new, sharp sound: the smashing of an axe into wood. Fowler was hacking a hole in his boat's hull just below the waterline.

Simon was already less than a hundred yards away. As he came closer he heard another sound: the yells and screams of the captive passengers below deck who now must see the axe blade and water breaking into the cabin where they were imprisoned.

The Saint pushed his throttle forward and bore down on the bigger boat at full speed, keeping his face hidden behind the black hat he was wearing. He turned on his own searchlight—a movable light that could be manipulated by the pilot at the wheel. In the beam he saw Fowler, a shotgun at the ready, facing the door from the cockpit and shouting over his shoulder:

"Hurry up! They're breaking out! Get me off here!"

The Saint obliged, and as he continued to race the last yards towards Fowler's listing boat he saw the doors burst open, wood splintering as the panic-stricken immigrants hurled themselves against it with a terror-inflamed vigour that Fowler had completely underestimated. Simon's timing was such that he managed to ram the cruiser at just the instant that Fowler pulled the trigger of his shotgun. The blast went harmlessly into the air instead of into the Indians and Pakistanis who now swarmed frantically and furiously over Fowler like ants from a disturbed nest.

"I'm a friend!" the Saint shouted to them. "Some of you can get in my boat. And throw over the rubber dinghy on the cabin trunk—you know, the roof. Keep calm! There's plenty of time for you all to get off."

Simon was trying to hold his own confiscated craft alongside the cruiser. The foreign passengers paused, confused and uncertain. Fowler was prostrate. Somebody appeared to be standing on his arm.

"I didn't exactly mean you've got all night," Simon called. "Come on—get that dinghy launched!"

There was a babble of English and other languages. Two of the men climbed over into the speedboat while others untied and pulled down the already inflated Zodiac. They shoved it headlong off the deck, making it ship a few gallons of water, but fortunately it was by nature unsinkable unless punctured in several places.

Then Fowler made a bad mistake: he rolled over and tried to recover his shotgun, which had fallen nearby. Simon had just time to prove the validity of his good intentions to the Indians and Pakistanis by levelling his pistol at Fowler, but he did not have to use it. Dark forms pounced in the dancing glare of the spotlight, and three knives entered Fowler's body almost simultaneously.

4

Fowler's boat was listing heavily stern down, but before the water began to spill into the cockpit the Zodiac was already loaded. If badly overcrowded, it at least floated. Nine men were in it, and three in the outboard with Simon.

"What happened?" one of the frightened passengers asked him. "Where are we?"

"The man who was supposed to take you ashore got frightened and decided to kill you instead."

He got his party organised, tying the raft behind so that he could tow it. Then he set out at a low speed towards the coast.

A shout went up, and he turned to look back. The lights of Fowler's cruiser had just disappeared beneath the waves, and the sea all around was dark except for the bead strings of lights along the distant shore.

Most of the way back to the vicinity of the fort was taken up by Simon's explanations to the smuggled aliens of just what had gone wrong to destroy their hopes—and almost to destroy them.

"Are you the police?" one of them asked.

"No."

"Where are we going? What can we do? Must we go to jail?"

"I'm afraid you must go back home," Simon told them. "As long as you don't go inside the territorial limits of Great Britain you haven't broken any laws. I'm going to leave you off at the fort you just came from. I'll arrange transportation so you can get back to the continent. You're on your own from there."

"I have no money!" one of them cried.

There was a scramble in the front of the boat.

"What is this?"

"I found it!"

The Saint's voice carried invincible authority.

"Give it to me," he ordered.

The packet which had caused the commotion was passed to him.

"It came from the man in the big boat," one said.

Simon looked inside. He did not need to count. The great thickness of the package was enough.

"What is it?" someone asked.

"How much did you pay for this outing?" the Saint asked.

"Five hundred pounds," one of them said.

"Four hundred," said another.

"Seven hundred!"

Simon interrupted.

"Before the bidding gets any higher, I am authorised by this packet to announce that your fares will be returned—at five hundred pounds a head, just to be equitable about it—on condition that you use part of the money to get back home and don't try any reverse colonisations in this direction in the future."

He kept the packet to himself until they arrived back at the fort. Then he sent all but the one most articulate of the men up the ladder from the boats.

"I'm going to give your comrades five hundred pounds for each of you," he said as they left. "Share it out equally, no matter what you paid to get here."

As he counted out the money from Fowler's package he told the Indian who had remained with him to assure the others that someone would come to take them away before noon the next day.

"Thank you, sahib." He looked wistfully towards the lights of the shore. "So that is all I shall ever see of England."

"Maybe you'll come back honestly some day. Or treat yourself to a two-week tour."

"Thank you, sahib."

He took the money, shook Simon's hand, and climbed up the ladder.

The Saint set the Zodiac adrift so that no over-enterprising immigrants could still use it to reach the coast, and scarcely had time to get the speedboat cast off and under way again when he heard a voice across the water.

"Ahoy there!"

The sail of the *Sunny Hours* was a white smear against the dark sky, cutting down swiftly towards him.

"Ahoy!" Simon said. "How do you know I'm not Fowler, about to put a bullet through your head?"

"I have faith in my Simon," Tammy called back. She steered to within a dozen yards of him, turning to luff into the wind. "When I heard the outboard coming back I knew it must be you. What happened?"

The Saint used a foot to fender their sides as the two boats drifted together.

"Kalki and Fowler are down among the dead men. Their clients just managed not to go with them. I'll tell you all about it on the way back."

"I'll race you," she said.

He looked at the luminous dial of his watch.

"I'll give you a tow," he said. "It'll save a lot of time, and old Nautical William back at South Benfleet is probably having kittens already about his precious scow. Besides, I'm starting to feel hungry for a real dinner . . . Curry, anybody?"

PUBLICATION HISTORY

The unusual origins of this story have already been explained, however it's worth noting that the TV episode which sprang from the original synopsis, written by Donald James and directed by Ray Austin, was first aired on Sunday, 22 December 1968.

The book was first published on 19 April 1971 as a Hodder paperback with a hardback edition being published over two years later on 28 August 1973. The first US edition appeared in 1972 and by 7 April of that year, Doubleday had sold 4,540 copies.

A Brazilian edition, *O Santo e as importações ilegais*, was published in 1972; an Italian edition, *Il Santo e i mercanti d'uomini,* in January 1975; a Dutch edition, *De Saint en de mensenhandelaren,* in 1972; and a Turkish edition, *İnsan tüccarlari,* in 1983.

ABOUT THE AUTHOR

I'm mad enough to believe in romance. And I'm sick and tired of this age—tired of the miserable little mildewed things that people racked their brains about, and wrote books about, and called life. I wanted something more elementary and honest—battle, murder, sudden death, with plenty of good beer and damsels in distress, and a complete callousness about blipping the ungodly over the beezer. It mayn't be life as we know it, but it ought to be.

—Leslie Charteris in a 1935 BBC radio interview

Leslie Charteris was born Leslie Charles Bowyer-Yin in Singapore on 12 May 1907.

He was the son of a Chinese doctor and his English wife, who'd met in London a few years earlier. Young Leslie found friends hard to come by in colonial Singapore. The English children had been told not to play with Eurasians, and the Chinese children had been told not to play with Europeans. Leslie was caught in between and took refuge in reading.

"I read a great many good books and enjoyed them because nobody had told me that they were classics. I also read a great many bad books which nobody told me not to read . . . I read a great many popular scientific articles and acquired from them an astonishing amount of general knowledge before I discovered that this acquisition was supposed to be a chore."[1]

One of his favourite things to read was a magazine called *Chums*. "The Best and Brightest Paper for Boys" (if you believe the adverts) was a monthly paper full of swashbuckling adventure stories aimed at boys, encouraging them to be honourable and moral and perhaps even "upright citizens with furled umbrellas."[2] Undoubtedly these types of stories would influence his later work.

When his parents split up shortly after the end of World War I, Charteris accompanied his mother and brother back to England, where he was sent to Rossall School in Fleetwood, Lancashire. Rossall was then a very stereotypical English public school, and it struggled to cope with this multilingual mixed-race boy just into his teens who'd already seen more of the world than many of his peers would see in their lifetimes. He was an outsider.

He left Rossall in 1924. Keen to pursue a creative career, he decided to study art in Paris—after all, that was where the great artists went—but soon found that the life of a literally starving artist didn't appeal. He continued writing, firing off speculative stories to magazines, and it was the sale of a short story to *Windsor Magazine* that saved him from penury.

He returned to London in 1925, as his parents—particularly his father—wanted him to become a lawyer, and he was sent to study law at Cambridge University. In the mid-1920s, Cambridge was full of Bright Young Things—aristocrats and bohemians somewhat typified in the Evelyn Waugh novel *Vile Bodies*—and again the mixed-race Bowyer-Yin found that he didn't fit in. He was an outsider who preferred to make his own way in the world and wasn't one of the privileged upper class. It didn't help that he found his studies boring and decided it was more fun contemplating ways to circumvent the law. This inspired him to write a novel, and when publishers Ward Lock & Co. offered him a three-book deal on the strength of it, he abandoned his studies to pursue a writing career.

When his father learnt of this, he was not impressed, as he considered writers to be "rogues and vagabonds." Charteris would later recall that "I wanted to be a writer, he wanted me to become a lawyer. I was stubborn, he said I would end up in the gutter. So I left home. Later on, when I had a little success, we were reconciled by letter, but I never saw him again."[3]

X Esquire, his first novel, appeared in April 1927. The lead character, X Esquire, is a mysterious hero, hunting down and killing the businessmen trying to wipe out Britain by distributing quantities of free poisoned cigarettes. His second novel, *The White Rider*, was published the following spring, and in one memorable scene shows the hero chasing after his damsel in distress, only for him to overtake the villains, leap into their car . . . and promptly faint.

These two plot highlights may go some way to explaining Charteris's comment on *Meet—the Tiger!*, published in September 1928, that "it was only the third book I'd written, and the best, I would say, for it was that the first two were even worse."[4]

Twenty-one-year-old authors are naturally self-critical. Despite reasonably good reviews, the Saint didn't set the world on fire, and Charteris moved on to a new hero for his next book. This was *The Bandit*, an adventure story featuring Ramon Francisco De Castilla y Espronceda Manrique, published in the summer of 1929 after its serialisation in the *Empire News*, a now long-forgotten Sunday newspaper. But sales of *The Bandit* were less than impressive, and Charteris began to question his choice of career. It was all very well writing—but if nobody wants to read what you write, what's the point?

"I had to succeed, because before me loomed the only alternative, the dreadful penalty of failure . . . the routine office hours, the five-day week . . . the lethal assimilation into the ranks of honest, hard-working, conformist, God-fearing pillars of the community."[5]

However his fortunes—and the Saint's—were about to change. In late 1928, Leslie had met Monty Haydon, a London-based editor who was looking for writers to pen stories for his new paper, *The Thriller*—"The Paper with a Thousand Thrills." Charteris later recalled that "he said he was starting a new magazine, had read one of my books and would like some stories from me. I couldn't have been more grateful, both from the point of view of vanity and finance!"[6]

The paper launched in early 1929, and Leslie's first work, "The Story of a Dead Man," featuring Jimmy Traill, appeared in issue 4 (published on 2 March 1929). That was followed just over a month later with "The Secret of Beacon Inn," starring Rameses "Pip" Smith. At the same time, Leslie finished writing another non-Saint novel, *Daredevil*, which would be published in late 1929. Storm Arden was the hero; more notably, the book saw the first introduction of a Scotland Yard inspector by the name of Claud Eustace Teal.

The Saint returned in the thirteenth issue of *The Thriller*. The byline proclaimed that the tale was "A Thrilling Complete Story of the Underworld"; the title was "The Five Kings," and it actually featured Four Kings and a Joker. Simon Templar, of course, was the Joker.

Charteris spent the rest of 1929 telling the adventures of the Five Kings in five subsequent *The Thriller* stories. "It was very hard work, for the pay was lousy, but Monty Haydon was a brilliant and stimulating editor, full of ideas. While he didn't actually help shape the Saint as a character, he did suggest story lines. He would take me out to lunch and say, 'What are you going to write about next?' I'd often say I was damned if I knew. And Monty would say, 'Well, I was reading something the other day . . .' He had a fund of ideas and we would talk them over, and then I would go away and write a story. He was a great creative editor."[7]

Charteris would have one more attempt at writing about a hero other than Simon Templar, in three novelettes published in *The Thriller* in early 1930, but he swiftly returned to the Saint. This was partly due to his self-confessed laziness—he wanted to write more stories for *The Thriller* and other magazines, and creating a new hero for every story was hard work—but mainly due to feedback from Monty Haydon. It seemed people wanted to read more adventures of the Saint . . .

Charteris would contribute over forty stories to *The Thriller* throughout the 1930s. Shortly after their debut, he persuaded publisher Hodder & Stoughton that if he collected some of these stories and rewrote them a little, they could publish them as a Saint book. *Enter the Saint* was first published in August 1930, and the reaction was good enough for the publishers to bring out another collection. And another . . .

Of the twenty Saint books published in the 1930s, almost all have their origins in those magazine stories.

Why was the Saint so popular throughout the decade? Aside from the charm and ability of Charteris's storytelling, the stories, particularly those published in the first half of the '30s, are full of energy and joie de vivre. With economic depression rampant throughout the period, the public at large seemed to want some escapism.

And Simon Templar's appeal was wide-ranging: he wasn't an upper-class hero like so many of the period. With no obvious background and no attachment to the Old School Tie, no friends in high places who could provide a get-out-of-jail-free card, the Saint was uniquely classless. Not unlike his creator.

Throughout Leslie's formative years, his heritage had been an issue. In his early days in Singapore, during his time at school, at Cambridge University or even just in everyday life, he couldn't avoid the fact that for many people his mixed parentage was a problem. He would later tell a story of how he was chased up the road by a stick-waving typical

English gent who took offence to his daughter being escorted around town by a foreigner.

Like the Saint, he was an outsider. And although he had spent a significant portion of his formative years in England, he couldn't settle.

As a young boy he had read of an America "peopled largely by Indians, and characters in fringed buckskin jackets who fought nobly against them. I spent a great deal of time day-dreaming about a visit to this prodigious and exciting country."[8]

It was time to realise this wish. Charteris and his first wife, Pauline, whom he'd met in London when they were both teenagers and married in 1931, set sail for the States in late 1932; the Saint had already made his debut in America courtesy of the publisher Doubleday. Charteris and his wife found a New York still experiencing the tail end of Prohibition, and times were tough at first. Despite sales to *The American Magazine* and others, it wasn't until a chance meeting with writer turned Hollywood executive Bartlett McCormack in their favourite speakeasy that Charteris's career stepped up a gear.

Soon Charteris was in Hollywood, working on what would become the 1933 movie *Midnight Club*. However, Hollywood's treatment of writers wasn't to Charteris's taste, and he began to yearn for home. Within a few months, he returned to the UK and began writing more Saint stories for Monty Haydon and Bill McElroy.

He also rewrote a story he'd sketched out whilst in the States, a version of which had been published in *The American Magazine* in September 1934. This new novel, *The Saint in New York*, published in 1935, was a significant advance for the Saint and Leslie Charteris. Gone were the high jinks and the badinage. The youthful exuberance evident in the Saint's early adventures had evolved into something a little darker, a little more hard-boiled. It was the next stage in development for the author and his creation, and readers loved it. It became a bestseller on both sides of the Atlantic.

Having spent his formative years in places as far apart as Singapore and England, with substantial travel in between, it should be no surprise that Leslie had a serious case of wanderlust. With a bestseller under his belt, he now had the means to see more of the world.

Nineteen thirty-six found him in Tenerife, researching another Saint adventure alongside translating the biography of Juan Belmonte, a well-known Spanish matador. Estranged for several months, Leslie and Pauline divorced in 1937. The following year, Leslie married an American, Barbara Meyer, who'd accompanied him to Tenerife. In early 1938, Charteris and his new bride set off in a trailer of his own design and spent eighteen months travelling round America and Canada.

The Saint in New York had reminded Hollywood of Charteris's talents, and film rights to the novel were sold prior to publication in 1935. Although the proposed 1935 film production was rejected by the Hays Office for its violent content, RKO's eventual 1938 production persuaded Charteris to try his luck once more in Hollywood.

New opportunities had opened up, and throughout the 1940s the Saint appeared not only in books and movies but in a newspaper strip, a comic-book series, and on radio.

Anyone wishing to adapt the character in any medium found a stern taskmaster in Charteris. He was never completely satisfied, nor was he shy of showing his displeasure. He did, however, ensure that copyright in any Saint adventure belonged to him, even if scripted by another writer—a contractual obligation that he was to insist on throughout his career.

Charteris was soon spread thin, overseeing movies, comics, newspapers, and radio versions of his creation, and this, along with his self-proclaimed laziness, meant that Saint books were becoming fewer and further between. However, he still enjoyed his creation: in 1941 he indulged himself in a spot of fun by playing the Saint—complete with monocle and moustache—in a photo story in *Life* magazine.

In July 1944, he started collaborating under a pseudonym on Sherlock Holmes radio scripts, subsequently writing more adventures for Holmes than Conan Doyle. Not all his ventures were successful—a screenplay he was hired to write for Deanna Durbin, "Lady on a Train," took him a year and ultimately bore little resemblance to the finished film. In the mid-1940s, Charteris successfully sued RKO Pictures for unfair competition after they launched a new series of films starring George Sanders as a debonair crime fighter known as the Falcon. But he kept faith with his original character, and the Saint novels continued to adapt to the times. The transatlantic Saint evolved into something of a private operator, working for the mysterious Hamilton and becoming, not unlike his creator, a world traveller, finding that adventure would seek him out.

"I have never been able to see why a fictional character should not grow up, mature, and develop, the same as anyone else. The same, if you like, as his biographer. The only adequate reason is that—so far as I know—no other fictional character in modern times has survived a sufficient number of years for these changes to be clearly observable. I must confess that a lot of my own selfish pleasure in the Saint has been in watching him grow up."[9]

Charteris maintained his love of travel and was soon to be found sailing round the West Indies with his good friend Gregory Peck. His forays abroad gave him even more material, and he began to write true-crime articles, as well as an occasional column in *Gourmet* magazine.

By the early '50s, Charteris himself was feeling strained. He'd divorced his second wife in 1943 and got together with a New York radio and nightclub singer called Betty Bryant Borst, whom he married in late 1943. That relationship had fallen apart acrimoniously towards the end of the decade, and he roamed the globe restlessly, rarely in one place for longer than a couple of months. He continued to maintain a firm grip on the exploitation of the Saint in various media but was writing little himself. The Saint had become an industry, and Charteris couldn't keep up. He began thinking seriously about an early retirement.

Then in 1951 he met a young actress called Audrey Long when they became next-door neighbours in Hollywood. Within a year they had married, a union that was to last the rest of Leslie's life.

He attacked life with a new vitality. They travelled—Nassau was a favoured escape spot—and he wrote. He struck an agreement with *The New York Herald Tribune* for a Saint comic strip, which would appear daily and be written by Charteris himself. The strip ran for thirteen years, with Charteris sending in his handwritten story lines from wherever he happened to be, relying on mail services around the world to continue the Saint's adventures. New Saint books began to appear, and Charteris reached a height of productivity not seen since his days as a struggling author trying to establish himself. As Leslie and Audrey travelled, so did the Saint, visiting locations just after his creator had been there.

By 1953 the Saint had already enjoyed twenty-five years of success, and *The Saint Detective Magazine* was launched. Charteris had become adept at exploiting his creation to the full, mixing new stories with repackaged older stories, sometimes rewritten, sometimes mixed up in "new" anthologies, sometimes adapted from radio scripts previously written by other writers.

Charteris had been approached several times over the years for television rights in the Saint and had expended much time and effort during the 1950s trying to get the Saint on TV, even going so far as to write sample scripts himself, but it wasn't to be. He finally agreed a deal in autumn 1961 with English film producers Robert S. Baker and Monty Berman. The first episode of *The Saint* television series, starring Roger Moore, went into production in June 1962. The series was an immediate success, though Charteris himself had his reservations. It reached second place in the ratings, but he commented that "in that distinction it was topped by wrestling, which only suggested to me that the competition may not have been so hot; but producers are generally cast in a less modest mould." He resented the implication that the TV series had finally made a success of the Saint after twenty-five years of literary obscurity.

As long as the series lasted, Charteris was not shy about voicing his criticisms both in public and in a constant stream of memos to the producers. "Regular followers of the Saint saga . . . must have noticed that I am almost incapable of simply writing a story and shutting up."[10] Nor was he shy about exploiting this new market by agreeing to a series of tie-in novelisations ghosted by other writers, which he would then rewrite before publication.

Charteris mellowed as the series developed and found elements to praise too. He developed a close friendship with producer Robert S. Baker, which would last until Charteris's death.

In the early '60s, on one of their frequent trips to England, Leslie and Audrey bought a house in Surrey, which became their permanent base. He explored the possibility of a Saint musical and began writing some of it himself.

Charteris no longer needed to work. Now in his sixties, he supervised the Saint from a distance whilst continuing to travel and indulge himself. He and Audrey made seasonal excursions to Ireland and the south of France, where they had residences. He began to write poetry and devised a new universal sign language, Paleneo, based on notes and symbols he used in his diaries. Once Paleneo was released, he decided enough was enough and announced, again, his retirement. This time he meant it.

The Saint continued regardless—there was a long-running Swedish comic strip, and new novels with other writers doing the bulk of the work were complemented in the 1970s with Bob Baker's revival of the TV series, *Return of the Saint.*

Ill-health began to take its toll. By the early 1980s, although he continued a healthy correspondence with the outside world, Charteris felt unable to keep up with the collaborative Saint books and pulled the plug on them.

To entertain himself, Leslie took to "trying to beat the bookies in predicting the relative speed of horses," a hobby which resulted in several of his local betting shops refusing to take "predictions" from him, as he was too successful for their liking.

He still received requests to publish his work abroad but had become completely cynical about further attempts to revive the Saint. A new Saint magazine only lasted three issues, and two TV productions—*The Saint in Manhattan*, with Tom Selleck look-alike Andrew Clarke, and *The Saint*, with Simon Dutton—left him bitterly disappointed. "I fully expect this series to lay eggs everywhere . . . the only satisfaction I have is in looking at my bank balance."[11]

In the early 1990s, Hollywood producers Robert Evans and William J. Macdonald approached him and made a deal for the Saint to return to cinema screens. Charteris still took great care of the Saint's reputation and wrote an outline entitled *The Return of the Saint* in which an older Saint would meet the son he didn't know he had.

Much of his time in his last few years was taken up with the movie. Several scripts were submitted to him—each moving further and further away from his original concept—but the screenwriter from 1940s Hollywood was thoroughly disheartened by the Hollywood of the '90s: "There is still no plot, no real story, no characterisations, no personal interaction, nothing but endless frantic violence . . ." Besides, with producer Bill Macdonald hitting the headlines for the most un-Saintly reasons, he was to add, "How can Bill Macdonald concentrate on my Saint movie when he has Sharon Stone in his bed?"

The Crime Writers' Association of Great Britain presented Leslie with a Lifetime Achievement award in 1992 in a special ceremony at the

House of Lords. Never one for associations and awards, and although visibly unwell, Leslie accepted the award with grace and humour ("I am now only waiting to be carbon-dated," he joked). He suffered a slight stroke in his final weeks, which did not prevent him from dining out locally with family and friends, before he finally passed away at the age of eighty-five on 15 April 1993.

His death severed one of the final links with the classic thriller genre of the 1930s and 1940s, but he left behind a legacy of nearly one hundred books, countless short stories, and TV, film, radio, and comic-strip adaptations of his work which will endure for generations to come.

> *I was always sure that there was a solid place in escape literature for a rambunctious adventurer such as I dreamed up in my youth, who really believed in the old-fashioned romantic ideals and was prepared to lay everything on the line to bring them to life. A joyous exuberance that could not find its fulfilment in pinball machines and pot. I had what may now seem a mad desire to spread the belief that there were worse, and wickeder, nut cases than Don Quixote.*
>
> *Even now, half a century later, when I should be old enough to know better, I still cling to that belief. That there will always be a public for the old-style hero, who had a clear idea of justice, and a more than technical approach to love, and the ability to have some fun with his crusades.*[12]

---

1 *A Letter from the Saint*, 30 August 1946
2 "The Last Word," *The First Saint Omnibus*, Doubleday Crime Club, 1939
3 *The Straits Times*, 29 June 1958, page 9

4 Introduction by Charteris to the September 1980 paperback reprint of *Meet—the Tiger!* (Charter), the last ever print edition.
5 *The Saint: A Complete History*, by Burl Barer (McFarland, 1993)
6 PR material from the 1970s series *Return of the Saint*
7 From "Return of the Saint: Comprehensive Information" issued to help publicise the 1970s TV show
8 *A Letter from the Saint*, 26 July 1946
9 Introduction to "The Million Pound Day," in *The First Saint Omnibus*
10 *A Letter from the Saint*, 12 April 1946
11 Letter from LC to sometime Saint collaborator Peter Bloxsom, 2 August 1989
12 Introduction by Charteris to the September 1980 paperback reprint of *Meet—the Tiger!* (Charter).

WATCH FOR THE SIGN

OF THE SAINT!

THE SAINT CLUB

And so, my friends, dear bookworms, most noble fellow drinkers, frustrated burglars, affronted policemen, upright citizens with furled umbrellas and secret buccaneering dreams that seems to be very nearly all for now. It has been nice having you with us, and we hope you will come again, not once, but many times.

Only because of our great love for you, we would like to take this parting opportunity of mentioning one small matter which we have very much at heart . . .

—*Leslie Charteris,* The First Saint Omnibus *(1939)*

Leslie Charteris founded The Saint Club in 1936 with the aim of providing a constructive fanbase for Saint devotees. Before the War, it donated profits to a London hospital where, for several years, a Saint ward was maintained. With the nationalisation of hospitals, profits were, for many years, donated to the Arbour Youth Centre in Stepney, London.

In the twenty-first century, we've carried on this tradition but have also donated to the Red Cross and a number of different children's charities.

The club acts as a focal point for anyone interested in the adventures of Leslie Charteris and the work of Simon Templar, and offers merchandise that includes DVDs of the old TV series and various Saint-related publications, through to its own exclusive range of notepaper, pin badges, and polo shirts. All profits are donated to charity. The club also maintains two popular websites and supports many more Saint-related sites.

After Leslie Charteris's death, the club recruited three new vice-presidents—Roger Moore, Ian Ogilvy, and Simon Dutton have all pledged their support, whilst Audrey and Patricia Charteris have been retained as Saints-in-Chief. But some things do not change, for the back of the membership card still mischievously proclaims that . . .

> *The bearer of this card is probably a person of hideous antecedents and low moral character, and upon apprehension for any cause should be immediately released in order to save other prisoners from contamination.*

To join . . .

Membership costs £3.50 (or US$7) per year, or £30 (US$60) for life. Find us online at www.lesliecharteris.com for full details.